GHOST TOWN

When the mining town of Silver Seam died, only Ray Ablett aimed to stay until the spring. The advent of a snowstorm drove a motley collection of individuals to seek shelter in the ghost town. There was a sheriff and his prisoner, a saloon girl, two buffalo hunters, a young Indian girl under the protection of the Kentuckian gunfighter, Jack Stone, and a Cavalry troop. When violence erupted, Stone needed all his deadly skills to secure his and the Indian girl's survival.

J. D. KINCAID

GHOST TOWN

Complete and Unabridged

LINFORD
Leicester

First published in Great Britain in 1994 by
Robert Hale Limited
London

First Linford Edition
published 1997
by arrangement with
Robert Hale Limited
London

British Library CIP Data

Kincaid, J. D.
    Ghost town.—Large print ed.—
    Linford western library
    1. English fiction—20th century
    2. Large type books
    I. Title
    823.9'14 [F]

    ISBN 0–7089–5046–9

Published by
F. A. Thorpe (Publishing) Ltd.
Anstey, Leicestershire

Set by Words & Graphics Ltd.
Anstey, Leicestershire
Printed and bound in Great Britain by
T. J. Press (Padstow) Ltd., Padstow, Cornwall

This book is printed on acid-free paper

To Jim and Elizabeth

1

WINTER had not yet relinquished its grip on the territory and icy winds continued to blow through the State of Nevada. It was mid-way through March, but snow still lay thick upon the plains.

The troop of bluecoated US Cavalry cantered through the snow as the sky lightened on that chill, bleak morning. They had been despatched from Fort McDermitt with orders to track down and eliminate a band of Shoshone renegades who had been rampaging through the plains east of the Trinity Mountains, murdering, raping and pillaging as they went.

The Shoshones' leader was a vicious, yet wily young Indian named Wolf's Tail. He had succeeded in eluding the law, in the form of the Army and various posses of US marshals, for a period of five years and more. But, finally, his luck had run out, and, two days earlier, the bluecoats had caught up with him and his renegade band and trapped them in a box canyon, in the foothills of the Trinity Mountains.

Wolf's Tail and his braves had put up a tremendous fight and, although outnumbered by four to one, had given a good account of themselves. They had been slaughtered to the last man, but had inflicted severe losses on the troop of US Cavalry. Five soldiers dead and nine wounded, four seriously, was the final tally.

Now, what remained of the troop was on its way back to Fort McDermitt. Its commander, Captain George Riley, was anxious to get the wounded back to the fort as soon as possible, yet the nature of their injuries prevented him from pushing on too fast. A tall, hawk-faced man in his late thirties, Riley was an experienced officer, a veteran of the Civil War and a renowned Indian fighter. He was respected, but not loved by his men, for he was an extremely harsh and ruthless individual whose cold, unbending manner did not invite affection.

Riley viewed the battle with Wolf's Tail and his braves as a success, though he could have wished to have incurred fewer casualties. He glanced at his second-in-command, Lieutenant Ben Nicholson, a youngster who had joined the regiment straight from West Point. He smiled thinly as he recalled the subaltern's conduct under fire. Nicholson had been frightened, of that he had no doubt, yet he had to concede that the young man had quickly conquered his fears and had done his duty. He did not like Nicholson, however, for he was prejudiced against all graduates from West Point, and Nicholson's easy manner, well-bred Bostonian accent and handsome, blond features irked him. Riley had come up through the ranks and he resented those who had not. High-faluting toffs who thought they were superior to ordinary mortals, was how he considered all West Point graduates. This attitude had not helped Riley's own career, which was why, at thirty-eight, he remained a captain. And his failure to reach the rank of major had left him embittered, and helped to make him the kind of man he was.

The bluecoats followed Captain George Riley northwards into the teeth of the wind. They struggled to maintain a good pace, for all were eager to return to the fort. Riley and the subaltern galloped on ahead and mounted the crest of a low hill, where they halted. Beneath them lay a small Indian encampment, the dozen or so tepees erected on a flat piece of meadow-land beside a meandering river.

"Paiute," said Riley tersely. He stared down at the camp with malevolent eyes and added, "They've strayed off the reservation."

"Are you sure?" asked Nicholson, for he was pretty certain that the Indian lands extended this far and beyond.

"'Course I am sure," snapped Riley.

"Wa'al, even so, they seem peacable enough," commented the lieutanant.

"You reckon?"

"Yes, sir. And I still maintain this is Indian territory, for aren't we looking down into Duck Valley?"

Riley coldly eyed his young fellow-officer. He knew, as well as Nicholson, that they were indeed overlooking Duck Valley, which formed part of the Paiute reservations. But he was not going to admit as much. He nursed an in-bred hatred of the red man, and was seeking an excuse, any excuse, to mount an attack upon them.

"I don't reckon so. An' I figure we got a duty to see those redskins don't stray," he said.

"But, Cap'n, they aren't doing any harm!"

"If 'n' they're outside their designated lands, then they're breakin' the law."

"So, what do you figure on doing?" asked Nicholson. "Don't forget, we have our wounded to consider. And I thought you were anxious to get them back to Fort McDermitt just as soon as possible?"

"So I am, Lieutenant, but this won't take no time at all."

"Then, you aren't planning to herd the Paiutes back to wherever it is you reckon they've strayed from?"

"Nope." Riley turned in the saddle and proceeded to address the troop. "Okay, men," he snapped. "We got ourselves a bunch of renegade Injuns here, who . . . "

"Hold on, sir, they're hardly renegades!" protested Nicholson.

"Are you questionin' my judgement?" demanded Riley.

"No, but . . . "

Lieutenant Ben Nicholson abruptly shut his mouth, silenced by his commanding officer's baleful glare. Riley turned again to the troopers.

"As I was sayin', men, we got ourselves a bunch of renegade Paiutes camped on the other side of this hill, an' it is the Army's duty to root out all such vermin," Riley smiled grimly, as he noted the looks of approval on the faces of the majority of his tough, battlehardened troopers. "Okay! So, my plan it this: Sergeant Collins, you will remain here with the wounded, while the rest of you men ride with the lieutenant an' me, down into that there encampment, an' give those red savages hell!"

"Yessir!" cried Corporal Joe Shaughnessy, the roughest and toughest man in the entire troop, a big, bloodthirsty ruffian who liked nothing better than killing Indians.

"An' remember, men, the only good Injun is a dead Injun!" added their captain.

Ben Nicholson was again inclined to protest, but he was too late, for, with a final "up an' at 'em!", Captain George Riley spurred his horse forward, over the crest of the hill, and immediately the troop galloped after him. Nicholson had no choice other than to ride with them. Behind him, the wounded sat shivering in their greatcoats, while Sergeant Frank Collins, a grizzled veteran, watched impassively as his comrades-in-arms bore down upon the Paiute camp. The sergeant was thankful to have been excluded from the raid, for, although he had happily participated in the destruction of Wolf's Tail and his renegade Shoshones, he had no wish to be involved in the massacre of the innocent Paiutes.

The Paiute village was inhabited mainly by women and children. The band was small in number and boasted only a dozen braves, four of whom were still in their early teens. They were totally unprepared for the bluecoated soldiers' sudden and unprovoked attack, and three of the braves were cut down before they could even arm themselves.

Two Elks, the young Paiute chief, tried to rally the other braves, but their lances and tomahawks were no match for the troopers' sabres, pistols and carbines.

Whooping and hollering, the US Cavalry charged through the camp, indiscriminately shooting and hacking down men, women and children. They gave no quarter and pursued their bloody business with an unholy glee. Mothers and babes-in-arms were hacked to death, young children riddled with bullets and the young men of the village either put to the sword or shot. The elders, men and woman alike, were summarily executed, while the younger women suffered an even worse fate. Urged on by their reckless, ruthless leader, some of the more depraved among the troopers jubilantly stripped and raped the young squaws before either stabbing or shooting them.

For his part, Captain George Riley revelled in the killing. He cut down Two Elks' beautiful young wife with a slashing blow from his sabre. Then, when Two Elks attempted to spear him with his lance, he fired a couple of shots into the Paiute chief's chest from point-blank range. The force of the two shots hurled Two Elks backwards and, as he lay flat on his back in front of his tepee, his two young sons, aged ten and twelve, ran out of the tepee and threw themselves down beside him. Laughing harshly, Riley rode up and emptied his revolver into the bodies of the children. Thereupon, he finished them off with a couple of vicious sabre slashes, practically decapitating the pair of them.

By this time, the soldiers had set the tepees alight and had massacred everybody except for three of four young squaws whom they were taking turns to rape. When, eventually, the troopers had had their fun and despatched the wailing woman with bayonet, sabre or bullet, Captain George Riley called the troop to order.

"Well done, men!" he cried. "That's sure put paid to these goddam red savages! But let's make certain there ain't no survivors. I want you to search in an' around this here Paiute village 'fore we leave."

The troopers, battle-crazed and filled with blood-lust, were, for the most part, only too willing and eager to search out any Paiute who might have slipped away, and they set about the task of searching the various surrounding patches of bush and scrub with an almighty zeal. There were a few, however, who had been sickened by the slaughter, and they were somewhat less enthusiastic. Among their number was the troop's second-in-command, Lieutenant Ben Nicholson.

He rode his black mare down to the water's edge, anxious to turn his back on the dreadful scene of desolation. Behind him, the once-peaceful Paiute village was littered with the bloodied corpses of its inhabitants, its tepees engulfed in flames.

As he trotted along the riverside, his face pale and his eyes troubled, Nicholson suddenly caught sight of a slight movement among the reeds which fringed a wide bend of the river. He urged his mare forward and, upon approaching the bed of reeds, found himself face to face with a small, buckskin-clad Indian girl. She was the thirteen-year-old daughter of the young Paiute chief, Two Elks. She stared out of the reeds at the subaltern, terror written all over her pretty young features. Nicholson attempted a sympathetic smile, but this did nothing to reassure the girl, who backed away, deeper into the reed-bed. Nicholson remained where he was. He had no knowledge of the Paiute tongue. The only way he could think of to communicate with the girl, was by means of sign language. Accordingly, he raised and pressed a finger to his lips. The girl's eyes widened in surprise. Did she understand? Nicholson had no time to find out, for, at that moment, the sound of hoof-beats crunching on the pebbles at the water's edge, warned him of an approaching rider.

The lieutenant quickly turned the mare's head and trotted across the shore-line to cut off the oncoming horseman. The newcomer was none other than Corporal Joe Shaughnessy. He clutched a blood-stained sabre in one hand and was evidently keen to find fresh victims.

"Found any more of them red savages, sir?" he enquired, taking a couple of practice swings with his sword.

"None, Corporal. I suspect we have killed them all," replied Nicholson.

"Yeah. Guess so, sir," growled Shaughnessy.

He promptly wheeled his horse round and headed back towards the burning Paiute village. Nicholson stole one last glance at the little Indian girl half-hidden in the reeds. Then, sighing heavily, he set off in the wake of the corporal.

Back in the village, Nicholson, who, by this time, had been joined by Sergeant Collins and the detail of wounded soldiers, reported to his superior officer.

"Wa'al, Lieutenant," said Captain

George Riley, "do you reckon we've accounted for 'em all?"

"Yessir, I do," replied Nicholson.

"Then, I propose we move on out. You ride with me at the head of the column. Sergeant, bring the men into line an', once that's done, take yore place at the rear."

"Very good, sir."

Sergeant Frank Collins snapped out a few succinct orders and the troop quickly formed up into a column of twos. Then, with the captain and the lieutenant riding at their head and the standardbearer riding immediately behind the two officers, the bluecoated horse soldiers resumed their long journey back towards Fort McDermitt.

★ ★ ★

Jack Stone had money to burn and was aiming to spend it either in Reno or in the state capital, Carson City. Six-foot two inches in his stocking feet and comprising two hundred pounds of

14

muscle and bone, the Kentuckian looked, and was, a formidable character. His craggy, square-jawed face bore witness to a life that had had its fill of ups and downs. Since being orphaned at the age of fourteen, Stone had endured both sorrow and hardship, had survived the Civil War and the turbulent years that followed, and had finally become a legend of the West as the man who tamed Mallory, the roughest, toughest town in all Colorado. Nowadays, though, he avoided trouble wherever possible.

Stone had spent the winter working on a ranch in Montana, having previously taken part in a cattle drive all the way up from Texas and on through Kansas, Nebrasaka and Wyoming. Now, with money in his pocket, he was looking to have some fun and relaxation. He crouched in the saddle, the brim of his grey Stetson pulled down low to shield his eyes from the biting wind that swept across the plains. He wore a thick sheepskin coat over his buckskins and was thankful for it.

As he peered across the snow-covered plain, the Kentuckian observed smoke rising from the far side of a low hill. He urged the bay gelding into a gallop. There was too much smoke for it to be coming from a single camp-fire, and Stone was curious to discover the cause. He mounted the rim of the hill and pulled up abruptly, his pale blue eyes glittering angrily as he surveyed the horrific scene that greeted him. He had seen that kind of carnage before, when he was serving as an Army scout, and it had sickened him. Whether the massacre in Duck Valley had been perpetrated by soldiers he had no means of knowing, but he rather suspected that it had.

Slowly, Stone trotted down into the village, threading his way between the burning tepees and carefully avoiding the bodies of the dead Paiutes. Men, women and children had all been indiscriminately butchered. The Kentuckian had not expected to find any survivors and, therefore, was quite surprised when, in the centre of the village, he found a small girl weeping silently beside the body of her father. He was more surprised when the body shuddered slightly. The man was not dead!

In fact, Two Elks was mortally wounded and had only survived this long because, with the bloodied corpses of his two young sons sprawled across him, the soldiers had assumed him to be dead and had not finished him off there and then. He turned his head as he heard the sound of the approaching horse's hooves. But he was quite unable to rise. Both he and his thirteen-year-old daughter stared stonily at the Kentuckian.

Stone dismounted and walked over to where the Paiute chief lay dying. Fortunately, he had, in his time as a scout, acquired some knowledge of various Indian languages and, so, was able to address the red man in his native tongue.

"Who did this?" he asked quietly.

"The bluecoats," replied Two Elks in a low, croaking voice.

"But why?"

"I do not know. Your government has signed a treaty agreeing that these are Paiute lands. And we have been living here peacefully for two or more years."

Stone nodded sombrely and then asked, "Is there anything I can do for you?"

He knew from experience that, should he report the massacre to the authorities, nothing much would be done. There might be some kind of enquiry and the officer responsible for the wanton destruction of the Paiute village would probably receive a reprimand. But that would be the most that could be expected. There was no real justice for the red man.

As Stone mulled over these grim thoughts and waited for the Paiute's reply, he suddenly became aware that the little Indian girl had slipped out of his line of vision. He half-turned, and saw that she had retreated a few paces and picked up her father's lance. There was hatred in her eyes, and he realised she was about to charge him and attempt to run him through. Surely he would not be forced to shoot her? His eyes met hers.

"Do not even think about it," he rasped.

Stone's remark caused Two Elks to glance towards his daughter. The dying Indian summoned up his dwindling strength and barked out a few words of command.

"Put down that lance!" he cried.

The girl glanced at her stricken father, but still clutched the lance.

"Put down that lance, Grey Dove," he repeated, his voice weaker, yet no less resolute.

The girl hesitated and then, finally, lowered the lance and dropped it onto the ground. Tears of frustration and despair coursed down her cheeks.

"Not all white men are bad, Grey

Dove; and I think this is a good man," whispered Two Elks.

"Thank you," said Stone.

"You asked if you could do anything for me," said Two Elks.

"Yes."

The Kentuckian crouched down beside the Paiute, for he could see that Two Elks was fading fast and he wanted to be sure to catch the man's dying words.

"I am Two Elks, chief of this small Paiute band and son of White Cloud," said the Indian.

"White Cloud, the Paiutes' tribal chief?"

"Yes. He lives with most of our nation on the reservation at Battle Mountain. I want you to take my daughter, Grey Dove, to White Cloud. Will you do this for me?"

Stone nodded. Battle Mountain lay in the direction from which he had just come, and a journey there and back would add quite a few days to his trip. But, then, he was in no particular hurry to reach Reno or Carson City, and, in any event, he could scarcely refuse the Indian's dying request.

"I'll do my best to make sure Grey Dove is delivered safely to her grandfather," promised the Kentuckian.

Two Elks smiled weakly. Then, he again turned his eyes towards his daughter.

"Grey Dove," he gasped, "you must trust this man."

"Yes, Father," replied the girl through her tears, but Stone could see that she remained extremely wary of him. It would, he realised, take time to convince Grey Dove that he meant her no harm.

"There is no need to be frightened. I will not . . ."

Stone, however, never completed what he had to say, for the girl suddenly screamed and threw herself sobbing across the chest of the Paiute chief. The Kentuckian glanced at Two Elks and saw that the Indian's eyes were staring sightlessly up into the sky. Stone promptly closed Two Elks' eye-lids and stood up.

He knew what he had to do. The Paiutes, like most of the tribes of the Plains Indians, traditionally placed their dead on wooden platforms until their flesh rotted away, and only then were their bones buried. Consequently, Stone gathered together as many poles as he could find, dismantling those few of the tepees which the bluecoats had failed to set alight. He hammered these poles into the ground and, using them as supports, he converted the Indians' travoises[1] into burial platforms.

This work took some hours and, by the time Stone had erected sufficient platforms to take the entire population of the village, Grey Dove had recovered sufficiently to help him. He placed Two Elks, his wife and two young sons on one platform and, at Grey Dove's

---

[1] A travois is a form of Indian sledge.

direction, laid out each Paiute family on a separate platform. This done, he and the girl covered the burial platforms with buffalo skins, which they then proceeded to secure with strips of rawhide.

"Okay," he said, "I think it is time for us to go."

Grey Dove nodded. She had become a little less nervous and a little more trusting as they had worked together. She still viewed the big Kentuckian with some timidity, but he sensed that she was beginning to accept him, if not as a friend, at least as a protector.

"My grandfather will come when the time is right and bury them," she said quietly.

"Yes,"

"But before we go, I should like to pray to the Great White Spirit."

"Of course."

The Kentuckian removed his Stetson and stood silently with bowed head, while the little Indian girl offered up a prayer to her god. Then, when eventually she had finished, he placed a large, comforting hand upon her shoulder.

"Right, Grey Dove," he said, "let us go."

Grey Dove looked up at him.

"You know my name," she said. "I do not, however, know yours."

"The name is Stone, Jack Stone," he replied.

"Pleased to meet you, Mr Stone," she said, and solemnly offered him her small hand.

He took it and smiled sadly.

"Pleased to meet you, Grey Dove, though I wish it could have been in happier circumstances," he replied.

While Stone mounted his bay gelding, the young Paiute retrieved her father's lance and then leapt onto the back of a small, piebald cayuse. She clutched the lance with one hand and gripped the reins with the other.

Stone eyed the lance warily.

"You won't need that," he said.

"It was my father's. I must take it

to my grandfather," said Grey Dove.

Stone shrugged his broad shoulders.

"Very well," he said and, turning the gelding's head, he set off at a canter, heading northwards across the seemingly endless plains in the direction of distant Battle Mountain.

Behind him rode Grey Dove, her father's lance held tightly in her left hand and tears of grief cascading down her cheeks. While she had been helping Stone prepare the burial platforms, she had succeeded in holding back her emotions. Now, however, she was finally leaving her village and her murdered family, and the full horror of the massacre struck her with fresh force. Her young heart threatened to break in two, so deep was her despair.

The man and the girl travelled on, their horses carrying them further and further away from the still smouldering tepees and the scene of desolation that had once been a happy, peaceful Paiute village.

2

THE small cattle town of Barton's Ford clustered on the eastern edge of Carson Lake. It consisted of one street, one hotel, one bank, one law office, a blacksmith's forge and livery stables, some cattle-pens, a small church, a small school, several stores, two saloons and a motley collection of adobe and white frame houses. A bitter wintry wind whistled through the town and, while the surrounding prairie-land was white with snow, the single thoroughfare through the town had been churned up into a black, glutinous quagmire.

It was into this uninviting spot that Roscoe Cutter and Billy Jackson rode on that chill March afternoon. The two men were cousins. They were also a couple of desperadoes, who had tried their hand at various nefarious occupations, but without much success. Their last venture had been a cattle-rustling raid upon the Double T ranch across the state line in California. Unfortunately for them, they had ridden straight into a large force of gun-toting cowboys and, as a result, the gang of rustlers had been badly shot up. Three had been killed and four wounded. Only the cousins had escaped unscathed and now here they were practically penniless, but safe from pursuit, in the State of Nevada.

Roscoe Cutter was three years older than his cousin. A brown Derby hat was clamped firmly on top of his head, and he wore a thick sheepskin coat over a much-patched check shirt and travel-stained denims. An ugly, heavily-bearded face peered out from beneath the brim of the Derby hat. His black eyes glittered fiercely as he surveyed the town, and he turned to his companion.

"Okay, Billy, reckon this'll do," he growled.

"For what?" asked the younger cousin, a thin, gangly youth, with a lean, pockmarked face and cold expressionless grey eyes. He was dressed similarly to Roscoe Cutter except that he sported a black, low-crowned, wide-brimmed Stetson in place of the other's Derby.

"For what? For makin' ourselves a li'l serious money," said Roscoe Cutter.

"In this one-horse town?" ejaculated Billy Jackson.

"It's a cattle town, ain't it?"

"So?"

"So, it's almost certain to have a bank."

"A bank! Hell, Roscoe, we ain't never done no bank robbery before!"

"We tried most things, Billy."

"Yeah, but not a bank! I dunno 'bout that."

"We're down on our luck, right?"

"Yeah."

"So, whaddya reckon we oughta do?"

"Wa'al, we got some experience of rustlin' cattle."

Roscoe Cutter could have pointed out that their experience in that field had been anything but successful. He forebore to do this, however, and simply contented himself with saying, "We'd need to recruit at least another four fellers to mount any kind of rustlin' operation. The two of us'd be no good."

"Hmm. Yeah, I reckon yo're right there."

"'Course I'm right. Therefore, hows about ridin' into this here town an' givin' the bank the once-over? If 'n' we don't like what we see, we can jest ride on out again."

Billy Jackson considered this proposal. It made sense and it committed them to nothing.

"Okay, I s'pose that cain't do no harm," he conceded.

"Then, let's mosey on into town," said Cutter.

He urged his sorrel forward and his cousin followed on his tan gelding. They crossed the town limits and trotted slowly through the morass that was the Main Street of Barton's Ford. They rode past the cattle-pens, the hotel, a couple of stores and the Cattlemen's Bank, one of the few two-storey buildings to grace the town.

The two cousins reined in their steeds on front of Macey's Saloon and dismounted. They hitched the horses to the rail and clambered up the steps from the street onto the stoop. They stood there for a few minutes, glancing up and down the deserted Main Street and taking particular notice of the bank on the opposite side of the muddy thoroughfare. Then Roscoe Cutter placed an arm round his cousin's shoulder and suggested that they enter the saloon and slake their thirst. Billy Jackson was quite happy to fall in with this proposal. So, they turned and pushed their way through the batwing doors, and stepped into Macey's Saloon.

The bar-room was sparsely populated, there being no more than a single poker game in progress and a solitary drinker standing at the bar. The drinker was an old saddle tramp who had seen better days. He was clad in grimy, tattered buckskins, and greasy, unkempt white hair sprouted out from beneath a disreputable racoon skin hat. His mottled, drink-sodden face was decorated with an untidy yellowish-white beard and whiskers, and he was smoking an ancient, foul-smelling pipe. The glass of whiskey on the marbled bar-top was evidently not his first, for he was by no means sober, as his bleary, red-rimmed eyes showed only too clearly.

"Afternoon, fellers," he said amiably. "I'd buy you both a drink only I'm down to my last few cents."

"In that case, have one on us," said Roscoe Cutter.

"That's mighty generous of you, sir," cried the saddle tramp, while Billy Jackson looked askance at his cousin.

Roscoe Cutter winked at the younger man, and proceeded to order three whiskies. Then, once the drinks had been poured, he raised his glass and proposed a toast.

"Yore good health, sir," he said.

"An' yore's," replied the old saddle tramp.

All three sank their drinks at one draught, whereupon Cutter ordered another round. Then he turned and offered his hand to the saddle tramp.

"My name's Roscoe Cutter, an' this here's my cousin, Billy Jackson," he said.

The old man shook the two cousins by the hand and favoured them with a crooked, drunken grin.

"Charley Skeets at yore service, gen'lemen," he croaked. "Anythin' I can do for you, you only gotta say."

Cutter studied the old man closely for a few moments before replying. "Mebbe Billy 'n' me could use yore help in carryin' out a li'l scheme we have in mind. But I'll need to discuss the matter with Billy, so if you'll excuse us for a couple minutes?"

"Sure thing," said Skeets.

Cutter grabbed his cousin by the arm and drew him across the bar-room to a table by the window. He placed his whiskey glass on the table and sat down. Jackson promptly followed suit.

"What the hell are you thinkin' of?" he demanded of Cutter in an angry whisper. "We cain't possibly use that drunken old fool. An', anyways, what li'l scheme are we s'posed to have in mind?"

Cutter glanced out of the window. Jackson followed his gaze and found himself staring directly across the street at the Cattlemen's Bank.

"Not that goddam bank!" he protested in a low voice.

"Why not?" demanded Cutter. "It's there for the takin'. The town's as quiet as the grave, an' we can be in an' out 'fore they know what's hit 'em."

"Hmm . . . Yeah . . . wa'al . . . I guess so," said Jackson, though without much enthusiasm.

"So, we'll do it? Okay?"

Billy Jackson sat silent for a while, quietly considering the matter.

"Okay," he said finally.

"Then, we'll need the services of Charley Skeets if 'n' we're to carry it of'," said Roscoe Cutter.

"But he'll be worse than useless. Hell, give him a gun an . . . !"

"We ain't gonna give him no gun. All we're gonna do is git him to hold the hosses ready for our getaway." Cutter nodded in the direction of the street and growled, "In case you ain't noticed, there ain't no hitchin' rail in front of the bank."

"We could leave our hosses tied up outside this here saloon."

"Then we'd need to cross Main Street on foot. You fancy runnin' through that morass? We'd git bogged down for sure."

"Wa'al . . . "

"I'm tellin' you, Billy, the only way is to ride over there, leave the hosses with Charley Skeets, then enter the bank an' do what we gotta do, an' hightail it outa town jest as fast as we can."

Billy Jackson glanced towards the bar-counter. The sight of the old saddle tramp slumped drunkenly over the marbled bar-top did not inspire him with confidence. Still, he reflected, all the old man had to do was hold the horses in readiness for their escape. Not a particularly difficult task.

"Reckon yo're right, Roscoe," he conceded. "We need the hosses right outside the bank if 'n' we are to make a fast getaway. So, I s'pose you'd best call the old feller over."

"Right." Roscoe Cutter grinned, and turned and called to the saddle tramp, "Okay, Charley, we've had our discussion. Why don't you come an' join us?"

Charley Skeets picked up his glass of whiskey and meandered unsteadily across to the table by the window. He collapsed onto a chair and smiled an inebriated smile at the two cousins.

"Wa'al, boys, are you proposin' to enlist my help?" he enquired, a gleam of curiosity entering his glassy, red-rimmed eye.

"We are," said Cutter.

"You got a hoss?" asked Jackson.

"Yup. She's hitched to the rail outside."

Jackson stretched his neck and peered out of the window. Apart from his and Cutter's steeds, there was only one other animal tied to the rail: a small, barrel-chested grey mare.

"Don't look much of a hoss," commented Jackson sourly.

"She's faster than she looks," retorted the saddle tramp.

"She'd better be," said Cutter.

"Why's that?"

"'Cause our li'l scheme is to rob that there bank across the street."

"Holy cow!"

"The idea scare you?" demanded Cutter.

"Nope. Jest surprised, is all," replied Skeets.

"So, whaddya say? Are you in?"

"I dunno. Y'see, I ain't got me no

hand-gun. I got an old Colt Hartford revolvin' rifle, but . . . "

"Don't worry. We ain't expectin' you to take part in the actual hold-up."

"No?"

"Nope. All we want is for you to hold our hosses, so's we can make a quick getaway."

Charley Skeets considered this for a few seconds. And, while he mused, he drank. Finally, he placed the empty glass on the table and, fixing a bleary gaze upon Roscoe Cutter, asked, "What's in it for me?"

"One tenth of whatever we git," said Cutter.

"One tenth! Huh, that ain't much!" exclaimed Skeets.

"Depends on what we git."

"Yeah, wa'al, however much it is, you an' yore cousin will be grabbin' nine-tenths. That don't seem fair."

"We're takin' all the risks. You'll only be tendin' to the hosses," replied Jackson.

"Which is vital if you fellers are to

make yore escape."

Roscoe Cutter cursed beneath his breath. The old fool might be drunk, but he wasn't so drunk that he had failed to observe the state of the town's one and only street and drawn the obvious conclusion.

"Okay," he said, "let's say an eighth."

"A third."

Billy Jackson laughed harshly.

"You gotta be jossin', old-timer. Like Roscoe said, you ain't takin' none of the risks," he rasped.

"Okay, mebbe I was bein' a touch greedy," growled Skeets. "Guess I'll settle for a fifth."

"One seventh," said Cutter.

"One sixth."

Cutter and Jackson exchanged glances. They had not expected the saddle tramp to drive so hard a bargain. Still, when it came to dividing the spoils, perhaps they could persuade him to be more reasonable. Or, if not . . .

"It's a deal," said Cutter, and the

three men shook hands.

"So, when are you folks aimin' to carry out this here robbery?" enquired Skeets.

"Now," said Cutter, draining his glass at one draught.

Jackson followed suit and the two desperadoes rose and immediately headed for the door. A slightly startled Charley Skeets staggered to his feet and hurried after them. His step was not as sure as he might have wished, yet he stayed on his feet, even after passing through the batwing doors and being hit by the chill, blustery wind that whistled through the town.

Both Roscoe Cutter and Billy Jackson climbed easily into the saddle, but Charley Skeets, adversely affected by the fresh air, seemed quite incapable of mounting his little grey mare. Eventually, Billy Jackson was forced to dismount and hoist the drink-sodden old-timer onto the mare's back. This accomplished, he climbed again into the saddle and glared angrily at his cousin.

"Are you sure we can trust Skeets to do his bit? Shouldn't we mebbe jest abandon the whole idea?" he demanded.

"No. He'll be okay. Won't you, Charley?" asked Cutter, smiling encouragingly at the saddle tramp.

"You . . . you may depend . . . depend on me," replied Skeets, with a drunken, lopsided and fatuous grin.

"The fresh air's havin' one helluva effect on him," commented Jackson.

"I know, but he's only gotta sit on his hoss an' hold onto the reins of ours," said Cutter.

"That's what's botherin' me," grumbled the younger man.

"Aw, c'mon, let's git goin'," said Cutter curtly, and he turned his sorrel's head and set off towards the bank.

The three riders progressed slowly through the thick, black mud to the opposite side of Main Street, where the cousins quickly dismounted and handed their reins to Charley Skeets. By this time, the saddle tramp was swaying dangerously, and Cutter reckoned it was only his high-backed Texas saddle that kept him from falling off the mare.

"Keep an eye open for the law," snapped Cutter.

"Sure thing," mumbled Skeets.

With one last, anxious glance at their drunken accomplice, Cutter and Jackson pulled up their kerchiefs to cover the lower part of their faces. Then they each grabbed a pair of saddlebags and clambered onto the sidewalk. Main Street remained deserted. That, at least, was good news. The two would-be bank robbers had left their Winchesters in their saddleboots, but each carried a Remington revolver in his holster. They drew these hand-guns and hurried into the bank.

The Cattlemen's Bank was empty of customers. Its busy period would be later in the year when the trail herd hit town. Business in the winter months was usually fairly quiet. The manager, a tall, distinguished-looking man in a grey frock coat, was sitting in his office reading a newspaper, while his young cashier, a pimply, bespectacled youth, was ensconced behind the counter, busily adding up a column of figures. Both men gasped with shock when Cutter and Jackson burst in on them.

"Okay, keep yore mouths shut an' don't try nuthin'!" cried Cutter, brandishing his revolver in front of the cashier's face.

"This . . . this is an outrage!" protested the manager, as he leapt to his feet.

"Yeah, wa'al, jest you put down that there newspaper an' come through here where I can see yuh," said Cutter.

"You . . . you'd best do as he says, Mr Simkins," quavered the young bank clerk.

"Yes. All right, jest you keep calm, Stanley," said Oscar Simkins, and he carefully laid down his newspaper and walked through into the main body of the bank. He stared stonily at the two robbers.

Cutter had to admire the man's nerve. Oscar Simkins was clearly not a man to be easily intimidated.

"Okay, Mr Simkins," said Cutter, "I want you an' yore clerk to fill these saddlebags with money."

"An' if we refuse?"

"Me an' my pardner, we'll shoot the pair of you."

"Hmm." Oscar Simkins eyed the saddlebags with a look of disdain.

"I ain't bluffin'," snapped Cutter.

"I . . . I guess we . . . we'd better do it," stuttered Stanley nervously.

The bank manager frowned, but still made no move to pick up the saddlebags which Cutter and Jackson had tossed onto the counter.

"Yes, I suppose so," he said at last, emitting a heavy sigh.

Stanley wasted no time, but began stuffing banknotes into one of Cutter's pair of saddlebags as fast as he could manage. At the same time, Simkins began filling one of Jackson's saddlebags, though with much less haste. Two of the four saddlebags were soon filled, and then Stanley began slipping coins into the third.

"Is that all the notes, you've got?" growled Cutter.

"Yes," replied Simkins shortly, though an anxious glance from the clerk to the manager told Cutter otherwise.

"You gotta safe?" he enquired.

"Wa'al . . . " began Simkins.

"Open it!" snarled Cutter.

At that moment, the door opened and a young woman stepped into the bank. She was small and petite, with dark brown hair and lively blue eyes, and she was wearing a dark blue velvet gown and matching bonnet.

Her sudden cry caused the two robbers to whirl round and, as they did so, Oscar Simkins made a grab for the scattergun which he kept loaded behind the counter. He was not quick enough, however, for, as he brought it to bear on Cutter, Jackson turned and fired. The forty-five calibre slug struck in the chest, smashing through bone and muscle and puncturing a lung. Simkins fell backwards and the shotgun was discharged harmlessly into the ceiling. A second shot, this time from Cutter, pierced the bank manager's forehead and blasted his brains out through the back of his skull.

The young woman screamed and, swivelling on her heels, made an attempt to escape through the open doorway. As she ran out onto the sidewalk, Billy Jackson fired twice. Both shots ripped into the brunette's back and passed through her body. She hit the sidewalk with a thud and lay twitching there, her life's blood slowly oozing away.

"C'mon, let's lam outa this town!" yelled Cutter.

He grabbed one pair of saddlebags and Jackson grabbed the other pair, and the two cousins sprinted out of the bank. Behind them, the young cashier cowered down behind the counter, badly shaken but unhurt.

They stepped over the body of

the dying woman and made secure the saddlebags before mounting their horses, the reins of which remained clutched in Charley Skeets' hand. He had given them no warning of the woman's approach, for he had fallen into a drunken stupor. Now, however, the sound of the shooting had woken him, and he was staring horrorstricken at the result of Billy Jackson's gun-play. He had been shocked into sobriety.

"Goddamit! You . . . you've gone an' murdered that young woman!" he exclaimed.

"Never mind that! Gimme my reins!" cried Cutter.

He and Billy Jackson both tore the reins from the old man's grasp and wheeled round their horses, ready to ride out of town. The shooting, though, had done more then simply waken Charlie Skeets. It had brought a goodly proportion of the citizens of Barton's Ford out onto the street. Armed with a variety of weapons and led by their sheriff and his deputy, they opened fire on the three miscreants.

Sheriff Daniel Budge, a tall, fair-haired young man in his middle twenties, was both courageous and conscientious. He had proved to be an exemplary law officer and he took his duties extremely seriously. Consequently, he came running along the sidewalk from his law office, shooting at the robbers as he ran. He had snatched up his Winchester and he emptied the rifle at the retreating figures.

Firing from the hip with a rifle is no easy task and a number of the young sheriff's shots missed their mark. But he recorded hits with three. Two struck Charley Skeets as he set off in the wake of his fleeing confederates. One caught the old saddle tramp in the thigh and the other in the shoulder, and they toppled him from his grey mare. He landed with a splash in the thick, black mud and, as he tried to stagger to his feet, a volley of shots from various of the town's citizenry cut him down.

47

The third of Daniel Budge's shots to find its target struck Billy Jackson in the left upper arm, ripping through his flesh and breaking the bone. The desperado managed to retain his seat, however, and he and Roscoe Cutter galloped hell-for-leather past the town limits. The townfolk of Barton's Ford continued to blaze away at the fast-departing gunslingers, but without success. Once clear of the town, Cutter and Jackson headed north along the snowbound trail, intending to make for and cross the state line into Oregon, where they had kin.

Back in Barton's Ford, a small crowd gathered outside the Cattlemen's Bank. Among their number were Daniel Budge, his deputy Dick Rogers, Norman Livesey who owned the Lakeside Hotel and was mayor of the town, Doc Hume, and the black-clad figure of the town's mortician, Oliver Daly.

It was Dick Rogers who first came upon the dead woman. He knelt down beside her and gently turned her over. Then he gasped with horror. The colour left his brick-red, weatherbeaten countenance. Middle-aged, overweight and easy-going, he had none of the sheriff's youthful enthusiasm. But he made an ideal deputy, giving Budge loyalty and support at all times. Now he was aghast, for the dead woman was none other then the sheriff's wife, Laura.

Daniel Budge, upon spying the lifeless body of his wife, let loose a cry of anguish and threw himself down and clasped her to his bosom.

It was some time before the sheriff could be prised away and, by this time, Oscar Simkins' corpse had been removed to Oliver Daly's funeral parlour and young Stanley, still very shaken, had been taken home to his family. Now it was the turn of Laura Budge to be taken and laid to rest in the funeral parlour. Daniel Budge refused any help and carried her there in his arms. He and Daly went inside, while the rest of the crowd remained outside on the sidewalk. Eventually, however, they began to disperse, some to their homes and some to one or other of the town's two saloons, there to discuss the event that had so suddenly and so violently disturbed the tranquillity of Barton's Ford.

Only the mayor and the deputy sheriff remained on the sidewalk outside the funeral parlour and, when presently Daniel Budge reappeared, the three men made their way together to the law office.

Once they had sat down, the mayor began by offering his condolences, but Budge cut him short.

"Thanks, Norm, but I ain't got time for that now," he said curtly.

Norman Livesey carefully scrutinised the young sheriff. He noted the man's unnnatural paleness, the drawn features and the tight lips. That Daniel Budge was exercising a great degree of self-control, and exercising it with much difficulty, the mayor had no doubt.

"What are you sayin', Daniel?" he asked quietly.

"I'm sayin' the sooner I git after them murderin' varmints the better," said Budge.

"You'll need to form a posse," said Livesey.

"No. I aim to track 'em down an' bring 'em in all by myself."

"But, Daniel . . ."

"My mind's made up."

"I'd willingly ride along with you," offered Dick Rogers.

The sheriff smiled sadly and shook his head.

"Nope," he said. "I want you to stay here in Barton's Ford an' make sure law 'n' order is maintained."

"Wa'al, if 'n' yo're sure?"

"I am."

"When do you intend settin' out?" enquired the mayor.

"Jest as soon as I've spoken with my children. Someone's gotta tell 'em what's happened to their ma, an' I guess it's down to me." Budge stared bleakly at the other two. "It ain't gonna be easy," he admitted.

"No." Norman Livesey cleared his throat and murmured, "While . . . while yo're gone, me an' Martha, we'll look after yore kids."

"Thanks, Norm, I'd'preciate that," said Budge.

"But what about Laura?" asked Rogers. "She'll needs be buried soon an . . . "

"I've asked Oliver Daly to pack Laura's body in charcoal. That'll help preserve her till I git back. Then we'll git the Reverend Brownlee to arrange a fittin' funeral service."

Daniel Budge's face was like a death-mask as he uttered these words. The very thought of packing his wife's body in charcoal sickened him, yet he knew that, if he were to catch up with her killers, he must set out without delay.

Accordingly, he went to the school, where he found his son and daughter, and broke the terrible news of their mother's death. This was easily the hardest thing Budge had done in his entire life. The second hardest was leaving them in the care of Norman and Martha Livesey, but he knew he had no option. Not if Laura's murderers were to be brought to book.

With his Winchester in the saddleboot and a Colt Peacemaker in his holster, Daniel Budge climbed onto the back of his rangy roan. He wore a grey Stetson and a thick sheepskin coat to keep out the bitter wind. Beneath the coat, attached to the pocket of his black leather vest, was the tin star, his badge of office.

As he cantered down Main Street, the whole town turned out to see him leave. But, although they all wished him success and a safe return, nobody cheered or clapped. The occasion of Laura Budge's death precluded any such demonstration. Instead, they simply watched in a respectful silence.

3

THE massacre of the Paiutes in Duck Valley and the bank robbery in Barton's Ford took place on the same chill March day. And, on the afternoon of that day, in the small farming township of Clinton Falls, half-way between Duck Valley and Barton's Ford, another drama was about to unfold.

It had begun the previous evening with Pete Sangster rolling off Sally McBride and announcing that he felt lucky. The pair had arrived in Clinton Falls a few hours earlier and had taken a room in the town's only hotel, Bates' Hotel. They had purchased a bottle of whiskey and taken it up to the room with them. Then had followed a bout of serious drinking and energetic lovemaking. Now they lay naked together in the untidy, sagging bed, happily replete.

They had been together for almost two years, the tall, handsome, black-haired gambler and the elegant, long-legged blonde. When his luck was in, Pete Sangster paid the bills and they lived the good life: the best hotels, the best restaurants, champagne by the bucket, the best seats at the theatre, in places like Reno, San Antonio, Denver and San Francisco. And, when he was down on his luck, Sangster simply put the girl to work. Sally McBride was what one might call a high-class whore. She didn't come cheap and she soon earned enough to stake Sangster at poker, or faro, or whatever game of chance he chose to play. Then, if he enjoyed another lucky streak, she ceased to be a sporting woman and kept herself solely for him. If, on the other hand, Sangster's luck remained out, then she once again plied her trade. In this manner, the pair had travelled the West. It was the kind of life that suited them both.

That evening Pete Sangster dressed with his usual care. He donned a crisp, white shirt, green brocade vest and dark, city-style suit. His string tie was almost brand-new and his highly-polished black shoes fairly gleamed. He strapped on his gun-belt, complete with a pearl-handled, forty-five calibre British Tranter, and stepped across and admired himself in the mirror.

Sally, meantime, sat up in bed, her large, firm, rose-tipped breasts peeping provocatively above the top of the bedclothes. She smiled encouragingly at the gambler and murmured, "You go on down, Pete, an' win us a real big pot."

Sangster grinned.

"Reckon I might jest do that," he drawled. "For, as I said, I'm sure feelin' lucky tonight."

"Good! I'll come down later an' see how yo're doin'. For now, though, I figure to git me some rest. Yo're one helluva active feller in bed an' consequently I'm plumb tuckered out."

Pete Sangster laughed and, crossing over to the bed, he bent down and kissed the girl. Tuckered out or not, she responded passionately and the gambler had some difficulty in extricating himself from her embrace. He was tempted to stay, but his desire to play poker was even stronger, for he had already enjoyed the girl's favours, whereas it was some days since he had last chanced his luck at cards.

And so it was that Sangster put on his grey Derby hat, left the hotel and crossed the street to the Alhambra Saloon, where he discovered and sat in on the biggest of the three games of poker in progress. It was a game that continued through the night, through the following morning and on into the early afternoon of the next day. And Pete Sangster was right. He did have a run of luck. He was several hundred dollars ahead when the final hand was played. By that stage, of the dozen players who had started on the previous evening, only five were left at the table.

Sangster glanced round at his fellow players. There was Jake Leary, the town mayor and a local storekeeper, a small, shifty-looking man in a rumpled three-piece suit; Doc Swann the local physician, a large, florid-faced fellow in a faded frock coat and battered stove-pipe hat; Nick Pearce, a lean, tough-looking rancher in buckskins and a white Stetson; and fourthly a buffalo hunter named Jim Wade, a huge mountain of a man, clad from head to toe in a variety of animal skins.

The final hand had been dealt and all but Doc Swann had discarded and drawn a single card. The doctor had discarded and drawn two cards. Now the bidding began. Jake Leary led and, as each man in turn called, the pot steadily increased. The first to quit was Nick Pearce. He threw in his cards the third time around. Jim Wade was the first to raise, but only by one hundred dollars. The others simply called and then Wade raised again, this time by two hundred. At this point, the mayor threw in his hand. This left the buffalo hunter, the doctor and Pete Sangster. The doctor and Sangster both called and waited for Wade to raise a third time, which he proceeded to do. They had guessed that he would, but had not anticipated that he would raise the stakes by quite so much. Five hundred dollars! He was either bluffing or he had one helluva good hand!

Doc Swann took a large swig of his whiskey.

"I'm in," he said quietly, after a little thought.

"Yore bet now, Sangster," growled Jim Wade. You gonna raise?" he enquired.

"Nope. I'll just call," said Pete Sangster, and he tossed the requisite number of greenbacks onto the pile in the middle of the table.

The buffalo hunter sat for a few minutes, contemplating his hand. Then, finally, he grinned and said, "I'll call, an' I'll raise you two thousand."

"Two thousand dollars!" ejaculated

the doctor. He threw down his cards with a flourish and declared, "Hell, that's a darned sight too rich for my blood!"

"What about yours, Sangster?" asked Wade.

Sangster glanced across towards the bar, where Sally McBride was perched upon a stool, drinking white wine and watching events. Over the last twenty or so hours, she had alternated between her hotel bedroom and the Alhambra Saloon, looking in from time to time to see how Pete Sangster was doing. Clad in an extremely low-cut red satin dress, she had quite brazenly flaunted her large white breasts and, by so doing, had succeeded in distracting one or two of Sangster's fellow players, a ploy she had used in various saloons in the past.

She was not, however, the only interested spectator. Jim Wade had a partner, one Larry Ince, a squat, pug-nosed, heavily-bearded fellow, whose clothing consisted of no less a variety of skins than did Wade's. He and Wade were on their way north to Oregon, where they intended to continue their buffalo hunting. And it was with their joint capital that Wade was gambling. Therefore, Ince looked more than a little anxious when his friend raised the stakes by two thousand dollars.

Both Sally McBride and Larry Ince waited with bated breath while Sangster deliberated.

He glanced at his cards. He held four jacks. Four of a kind. The odds against his opponent holding a similar number of queens, kings or aces were pretty damned high. Therefore, to beat him, Jim Wade would need to have either a straight flush or a royal flush. And the odds against him holding either of those hands were even higher. So, why had Wade raised by such an extravagant sum? Was he simply bluffing and hoping, by making such a bid, to force his opponents into folding? If so, he had certainly succeeded with

Doc Swann. But Sangster was made of sterner stuff.

There was, of course, the possibility that Wade was double bluffing, that he wanted Sangster to think he had a comparatively poor hand, while all the time he held a good one. Sangster smiled inwardly while remaining outwardly inpassive. If that were the case, he should still win, for he could not imagine the buffalo hunter holding a better hand than his own.

Sangster, as a professional gambler, calculated that he ought, in all probability, to raise. But there was a snag. He did not have the cash. Therefore, he would have to content himself with simply seeing the other's hand.

"I'll see you." he said.

"Cash on the table." growled Jim Wade.

"Okay."

Pete Sangster had so far played shrewdly and been lucky, and he had accumulated a decent amount of winnings. But, up until the present hand, the stakes had been moderate. In consequence, Sangster found that he was two hundred and twenty dollars short.

"That all you got?" growled the buffalo hunter. "Wa'al, in that case, I reckon the pot's mine, for if 'n' you cain't raise the two thousand, you don't see."

"Wait a minute," snapped Sangster. He turned to face Sally McBride, who had put down her drink and was gazing wide-eyed at the poker table. "Sally, how much have you got?" he demanded.

"How much do you need?" asked the blonde.

"Two hundred and twenty dollars," interjected Jim Wade, with a grin.

The girl scabbled feverishly inside her reticule and produced a few notes and a scattering of coins.

"That's all I've got," she said, and stepped across and handed the money to her lover.

He slowly counted it out onto the table. It came to exactly eighty-four dollars and fifty cents.

Larry Ince laughed and said, "Pick up the pot, Jim. Guess Mr Sangster ain't gonna make it."

"Okay, so I'm outa cash. But I got me a genuine gold hunter, an' that's surely worth a few dollars?" said Sangster, pulling the watch from his vest pocket.

"Not to me it ain't. I don't need no time-piece," said Wade.

"Wa'al, I have a buggy an' a pair of good, finely-bred mares over at the livery stables. You can have them instead of the hundred an' thirty-five dollars an' fifty cents I'm short."

"No deal."

"Gimme a break. Let me see what I can raise on 'em."

"The rules are clear. You leave this table an' the hand's mine."

"But, hell . . . !"

"Wade's right. Those are the rules," said Jake Leary.

He and Nick Pearce had remained in their seats, and were watching the unfolding drama with great interest. Poker in Clinton Falls was not usually as exciting as this. Normally, the stakes were fairly low. Neither could recall a bet of two thousand dollars being made before. That was the kind of gamble one might expect to be undertaken by high-rollers in places like Reno or 'Frisco.

The other patrons of the Alhambra Saloon had by now gathered round, all anxious to see the conclusion of the game. They were all willing Pete Sangster to find the money needed to see Jim Wade's hand, for, if, through lack of funds, he had to fold, that would indeed be an anti-climax.

"The woman yourn?" enquired one of them, a short, bald-headed fellow. He jerked his head in Sally McBride's direction.

Sangster nodded.

"Then, put her up. Reckon she's worth a hundred an' thirty-five dollars of anyone's money."

Jim Wade looked up from his cards and glanced across at Larry Ince. The smaller buffalo hunter leered at the girl, his eyes running lasciviously over her voluptuous body. He stroked his beard and grinned broadly.

"That's okay by me, Jim," he drawled.

"Right," said Wade. "You wanta see me, I'll take the woman in lieu of yore shortfall."

"Hell, no!" exclaimed Sangster. "You cain't have both her an' the money I put down. It's one or the other."

"You puttin' a price on me?" said Sally.

"I'm jest sayin' yo're worth more 'n a measly hundred an thirty-five dollars."

"Not to me, she ain't," stated Wade.

"But . . . " began Sangster.

"It'll take what you've already put down on the table, plus the woman, to see me. An' that's my final word."

Sangster could see that the buffalo hunter meant what he said, and it was

Wade who was calling the shots. He either had to agree, or he had to quit.

"Okay," he said, between gritted teeth.

"No!" cried an ashen-faced Sally McBride. "I ain't yourn to sell! I ain't nobody's to sell!"

"Trust me, Sally," said Sangster. "I ain't gonna lose this hand."

Sally stared fearfully at the gambler. She had supported him by selling her body in various saloons and bordellos across the West, but that was quite different from becoming the property of a couple of rough and ready buffalo hunters, to do with as they wished for as long as they wanted her. She could imagine her fate on the long journey into Oregon, and the very thought filled her with terror and revulsion.

"No," she said.

"Sally, I'm tellin' yuh, I ain't gonna lose," he repeated firmly.

The girl hesitated. Pete Sangster was a cool customer and a good card-player. For him to be so confident, he had to have a very good hand indeed. She stared at the pile of money in the centre of the poker table. It was certainly a pot worth winning. She continued to hesitate, but, in the end, avarice scored over caution.

"All right," she said, in a low voice, although all the colour had faded from her face and she was hard put not to tremble.

"Okay, Wade," said Sangster. "Let's see what you've got."

Jim Wade grinned and turned over the two of hearts. This was followed by the three, the four and the five, all of the same suit. At this point, he paused, deliberately building up the suspense. Had he been bluffing or did he hold the six of hearts?

The final card flipped over. Jim Wade had not been bluffing. Pete Sangster stared down at the six of hearts. The incredible had happened. The buffalo hunter held a straight flush. Sangster calculated that the odds, against a straight flush and four of a kind both turning up in the same game, must be several thousand to one.

"You . . . you said you weren't gonna lose!" Sally cried accusingly.

"Hell, it was close on impossible!" exclaimed the gambler.

"Wa'al, that's the way it goes sometimes," said Wade, as he proceeded to gather up the money from the table.

At the same time, Larry Ince stepped up behind the girl and grasped her firmly by the arm.

"Guess you'll be comin' along with us," he hissed, digging his fingers into her soft, white flesh.

Sally winced and gasped, "This . . . this ain't right. I . . . I don't belong to you. I don't belong to nobody!"

"You agreed to the deal," retorted Ince.

"But we fought a civil war to abolish slavery!" she protested. "Surely you won't let 'em take me?" she demanded of Clinton Falls' mayor.

69

Jake Leary shrugged his shoulders.

"Seems to me you entered into a contract when you agreed to let Sangster put you up as collateral," he said quietly.

"No! I won't go! I won't . . . aaah!"

A vicious slap across the face silenced the blonde's protests and left a deep red imprint on her pale cheek. Larry Ince pushed his cruel, bearded features close to hers.

"You can come nice 'n' easy, of yore own free will," he rasped. "Or you can come strugglin'. But, if you come strugglin', yo're sure as hell gonna git hurt."

Sally held back her tears with some difficulty. She had her pride and she wasn't about to let anyone present see her cry. There was evidently no help coming from the citizens of Clinton Falls. As far as those sonsofbitches were concerned, she had made her bed and she must lie in it. Therefore, she turned her gaze upon the man who got her into this mess.

"Wa'al, Pete, ain't you got nuthin to say?" she asked tremulously.

Pete Sangster pulled a wry face.

"Don't worry, honey, I'll win you back somehow," he promised.

"Oh, yeah?" sneered Jim Wade. "Whaddya think yo're gonna bet with? Buttons?"

An explosion of laughter rippled through the crowd round the table, and Sangster flushed with anger.

Sally, however, was one person who did not laugh. She knew that Sangster was her only hope. But his reply had been downright discouraging. How could he possibly raise the wherewithal to challenge the buffalo hunter to another game of chance? And even if, by some miracle, he did, who was to say he would win? Sally's feeling of despondency deepened.

"C'mon, girl. It's time we hit the trail," said Larry Ince, tightening his grip on her arm.

"Yeah. Cain't hardly wait to git started," said Jim Wade, gazing at the blonde with hot, lustful eyes. "There ain't no woman where we're goin', so usually we have to wait till we return to civilisation 'fore we can have us some fun. But not this time. No, sirree, this time we're takin' along our own personal whore!"

"That's right, Jim," agreed his partner. "We're sure gonna have ourselves a good time on this trip!"

The two buffalo hunters chuckled and then bundled the blonde out of the saloon. Nobody made any attempt to stop them, not even Pete Sangster. As the trio pushed through the batwing doors, Sally turned her head and directed one last, despairing gaze at the gambler. Then she was gone. Sangster threw back the remains of his whiskey and picked up his grey Derby hat. He slapped it on his head and headed slowly towards the door.

He remained on the stoop outside the Alhambra Saloon and watched the buffalo hunters make their preparations for departure. As he watched, Larry

Ince took Sally McBride across the street to Bates' Hotel to collect her few belongings, while Jim Wade hitched a couple of mules to their covered wagon and loaded it with provisions. In this last exercise, Wade had the help of Jake Leary, whose general store he was patronising. When Larry Ince returned, he threw Sally's baggage into the rear of the wagon and tied her to it with a short length of rope. Then, he proceeded to help the others with the loading. Sangster continued to watch and, by and by, he dropped his right hand onto the pearl-handled butt of his British Tranter. At that moment, a quiet yet firm voice whispered in his ear.

"I wouldn't if I was you."

Sangster whirled round to find himself face to face with a short, dapper man in a long black coat and black Stetson. The man was carrying a Colt Peacemaker in his holster, and the badge on his vest proclaimed him to be town marshal.

"I . . . I wasn't aimin' on doin' nuthin'," muttered Sangster, hastily withdrawing his hand from the butt of his gun.

Marshal Bob Taggart eyed the gambler closely and permitted himself a wintry smile.

"I heard 'bout the game an' how you lost yore woman to them two buffalo hunters," he drawled.

"Yeah."

"You try shootin' it out with 'em an' I reckon you'll git yoreself killed."

"Mebbe."

"Anyways, I don't want no shootin' here in Clinton Falls."

"No, Marshal."

"You follow 'em out onto the plains an' tackle 'em there, that's yore business. Jest so long as it's outa my jurisdiction. Do I make myself clear?"

"As crystal."

"Okay." Taggart drew on the large, fat cigar, which he had planted between his lips, and added, "A word of advice.

Odds of two to one ain't good."

"So?"

"So, you'll need to catch 'em by surprise. An' them buffalo hunters are gonna be half-expectin' you to track 'em an' try somethin'. They'll be on their guard for at least the first few days. Therefore, I wouldn't rush things."

"Lull 'em into a false sense of security, huh?"

"Somethin' like that."

"Why are you tellin' me this, Marshal?" asked Sangster curiously.

"'Cause the woman deserves a better fate than bein' tied to them couple roughnecks for months on end. Hell, they ain't gonna be too partickler how they use her!"

"You could order 'em to release her."

The lawman laughed harshly.

"Nope. They ain't breakin' no law as I'm aware of. The li'l lady agreed to put herself up as part of yore bet." Taggart shrugged his shoulders. "A goddam foolish thing to do, yet I

75

reckon the price she's likely to pay for that mistake is rather too high."

"Yeah."

"Anyways, I'd advise you to use stealth rather than gun-play. Sneak her away one dark night when they're snorin' their heads off," suggested the marshal.

"That's easier said than done."

"Sure, but, as I said earlier, you try shootin' it out with 'em an' you could git killed. An' where would that leave the li'l lady?"

Pete Sangster nodded. The marshal had a point. He was no gunslinger and, in all likelihood, would not survive a gunfight with the two buffalo hunters. What was needed was a shrewd mixture of caution and guile. He would follow the buffalo hunters' wagon, but only make his move when he thought he had a good chance of success. And he would resort to using his British Tranter only if forced to do so.

"Thanks for yore advice, Marshal," he said "I'll bear it in mind."

Taggart smiled and carried on down the sidewalk. Sangster watched him go and then reverted his gaze to the covered wagon. It was fully loaded by now and Larry Ince had untied the blonde and was helping her up onto the buckboard. He clambered up behind her. With Jim Wade on one side of her and Larry Ince on the other, there was to be no chance of escape.

Wade took hold of the reins and set the mules trotting off down Main Street. The wagon rumbled through the muddy throughfare, the buffalo hunters' eyes glued to the trail ahead, while Sally McBride turned and stared back at her erstwhile lover. Her pale face was a picture of despair, her large blue eyes brimming with unshed tears.

Pete Sangster cursed, and turned and headed for the livery stables. There he sold the buggy and bought a couple of saddles, which he slung across the backs of his two black mares. When he had tightened the girths, he mounted one mare and, leading the other on a short rein, cantered out of the livery stables.

By the time he had passed beyond the town limits, the wagon was no longer in view, hidden by a bend in the trail. Sangster smiled thinly. He would follow at a distance, taking care not to be spotted by his quarry. He shivered. The bitter March wind cut sharply through his city-style suit and green brocade vest, and he wished that he had thought to purchase a thick coat. But there was no going back. He gritted his teeth and continued along the trail.

4

DARK clouds scudded across the mid-day sky. It was the day following the massacre at Duck Valley and Grey Dove had by now come to trust the Kentuckian. Her father's command that she do so, and Stone's subsequent behaviour towards her, had eventually won her over. They had worked together, they had ridden together, and they had spent a night sleeping together beside a blazing camp-fire. And, during all of this time, Stone had sought only to comfort and protect her.

Glancing up into the sky, Stone addressed Grey Dove in her native tongue.

"I fear that we may be in for a storm," he said.

Grey Dove peered anxiously at the ominous black clouds.

"A snow-storm?" she said.

"Yes."

As he spoke, they mounted a small rise. Ahead of them, a quarter of a mile away, was a stand of cottonwood. At the edge of the wood Stone spotted a covered wagon and two mules. The mules had been unhitched and were grazing contentedly on the coarse, spiky grass of the plain, while two men huddled over a small fire, drinking coffee. A third figure stood alone, close to the wagon.

Stone narrowed his eyes. The third figure was that of a young woman. She was blonde-haired and beautiful and, as the Kentuckian and the Paiute girl rode closer, he observed that she was tied to the wagon. The rope attached to her left wrist was clearly visible.

The two buffalo hunters rose to their feet and stared at the Kentuckian and his diminutive companion.

"Howdy, stranger," said Larry Ince. "You care to stop for some coffee?"

"I don't think so," said Stone.

"That there Injun gal, is she some kinda servant?" enquired Jim Wade curiously.

"Nope. I'm taking' her to her grandpa on the reservation at Battle Mountain."

"How come?" demanded Ince.

"'Cause her pa asked me to."

"You runnin' errands for Injuns?" ejaculated Jim Wade.

"Her pa is dead. He an' his entire village was massacred back along the trail at Duck Valley," explained Stone.

"Hmm." Larry Ince had no great love of Indians, so the news of the massacre did not bother him unduly. However, he guessed that Stone held a different viewpoint and, recognising that the Kentuckian was not a man to cross, he wisely decided against making any comment. Instead, he confined himself to saying quietly, "Wa'al, I guess it's yore business what you do."

"Yup." Stone glanced across at Sally McBride, tethered like a goat to the wagon. " You usually keep yore women

81

tied up?" he asked idly.

"We won her fair an' square in a poker game," said Larry Ince.

"She offered herself as collateral, an' now she's regrettin' it, an' keeps tryin' to run off. She's tried twice since we set out, so we got no choice but to keep her tied up," added Jim Wade.

"That true?" Stone asked the blonde.

Sally nodded, her eyes downcast.

"I guess so," she sighed. "The feller I was with reckoned he couldn't lose, but he was one hundred an' thirty-five dollars short of the amount needed to see that big lunkhead's hand."

"An' you offered yoreself in lieu?"

"Pete was sure he'd win."

Stone smiled wryly. Where had he heard that before? His father had lost the family farm through gambling, and Stone had, in his time, encountered several others ruined by their addiction to cards or dice. Stone was no gambling man and never would be.

"Wa'al," he said, "I reckon Pete was a fool, an' you were an even bigger one."

"I admit it, but do I deserve this?" cried Sally.

"Nope, don't reckon you do." Stone turned to face the two buffalo hunters. "Untie her," he said quietly. "This ain't no way to treat a woman, even if she does threaten to run off."

"An' who the hell d'you think you are to tell us what to do?" demanded Wade.

The Kentuckian stared hard at the two men, his pale blue eyes glittering angrily.

"Name's Stone. Jack Stone. Mebbe you've heard of me?"

Jim Wade gulped. He had heard of Stone all right. The man was a legend, a gunfighter of matchless courage and ferocity. When the chips were down, there was nobody deadlier than Stone.

"Er . . . .. pl . . . pleased to meet you you, Mr Stone," he stammered. "My name's Jim Wade, an' this here's my pardner, Larry Ince."

"Yeah . . . er . . . pleased to meet you, Mr Stone," said Ince, for he, too, knew of the Kentuckian's fearsome reputation.

"You gonna untie the woman?" rasped Stone.

"Er . . . yeah . . . sure thing, Mr Stone," said the smaller of the two buffalo hunters, and he hurried across and hastily began to undo the rope holding Sally to the wagon.

"Thank you, Mr Stone," said Sally, rubbing the circulation back into her wrist.

"My pleasure, Miss . . . er . . . "

"McBride's the name, but you may call me Sally."

"Yeah. Wa'al, my advice is, you stick with these two fellers, at least for the present. If 'n' you try runnin' off' yo're liable to freeze to death."

"Whaddya mean, Mr Stone?"

"I mean, Miss Sally, that there's a storm a-comin', an' it promises to be a pretty goddam fierce one. You git caught out in it an' yo're dead for sure."

Jim Wade glanced up at the darkening sky. He scowled.

"Reckon we'd best git everythin' tied down, then," he muttered.

Stone glanced at the covered wagon and shrugged his brawny shoulders.

"That there wagon ain't in too good shape," he said. "The canvas is poorly patched an' even torn in places. A real strong wind'll tear that to shreds."

"So, whaddya suggest?" demanded Wade.

"There's a small silver-minin' town 'bout a coupla miles north of here. Reckon, if you move out now, you could reach it 'fore the storm breaks," said Stone.

"Then, what are we waitin' for?" cried Ince.

He and Wade immediately set about breaking camp and hitching the mules to the wagon. Within five minutes, they and the girl were up on the wagon and following Stone and his small companion northwards.

Overhead, the storm clouds continued to gather. At the same time, the wind increased in ferocity and the travellers lowered their heads and battled on into the teeth of the gale.

During the course of their journey together, Stone had learned that Grey Dove spoke no English. Consequently, she could have little or no idea of what had been said.

"Do not worry. There is a town nearby. We shall shelter there," he explained to her, shouting to make himself heard.

Grey Dove smiled.

"I do not worry. I am with you," she said simply.

Those two miles seemed to take an eternity to cover, but, eventually, they rounded a high bluff and found themselves entering a wide, shallow valley, in the centre of which stood a small cluster of wooden shacks and other buildings. A rickety signpost indicated that the township was called

Silver Seam. It consisted of but a single street and appeared to be quite deserted. Indeed, the only movement came from the tumbleweed, which was being blown through the town by the bitter, gale-force wind.

"Hell, it's a goddam ghost town!" exclaimed Jim Wade.

"Sure is," agreed Stone. "Guess the silver ran out an' the folks jest moved on."

"So, what in tarnation do we do now?" asked Larry Ince.

"We find ourselves some shelter. We can mebbe stable the hosses an' the mules, an' find some place to stow away the wagon," said Stone.

"Wa'al, we'd better hurry, for it's startin' to snow," said Sally.

This was true. The first flakes were beginning to fall and, the wind being as fierce as it was, it could only be a matter of minutes before a full-scale blizzard was raging. Consequently, they quickened their pace and entered the township at a canter. Then, all at once, they noticed the flood of yellow light that spilled out onto the sidewalk half-way down the street, escaping from the door and ground-floor windows of the town's one and only two-storey building, the Silver Dollar Saloon.

As they approached the saloon, the batwing doors were pushed open and a small, wiry man, in shirtsleeves and with his trousers held up by bright red suspenders, stepped out onto the stoop. He was dark-haired and had a lean, narrow face, sad, brown eyes and a long, drooping moustache. His sad eyes lightened as he observed the new arrivals in town, and he greeted them with a warm, welcoming smile.

"Welcome to Tumbleweed City," he said. "Y'all best come in 'fore this storm really gits a grip."

"Glad to," said Stone. "But you got anywheres we can stable our hosses an' mules an' stow away this here wagon?"

"Sure thing. There's stables an' a barn round the back," said Silver

Seam's one and only citizen.

Stone immediately took command and, while Larry Ince escorted Sally McBride and Grey Dove into the saloon, the Kentuckian and Jim Wade proceeded to stable and unsaddle the horses and unhitch and stable the mules. The wagon they locked away in the safety of the barn. Large and commodious, it already held another wagon and was also home for another couple of mules, one cow, one pig and half a dozen chickens.

This and the stables were easily reached by way of a narrow passage between the Silver Dollar Saloon and a building that had once been Silver Seam's barbering parlour. However, by the time they had completed their task, the two men found that a full-scale blizzard was raging outside. They did not, therefore, go back up the alleyway and enter the saloon from Main Street. Instead, they dashed from the stables, across a small yard and through a door into the rear of the saloon, where they found themselves in the kitchen.

From the kitchen they proceeded along a short, narrow passage and on into the bar-room. Here they were re-united with their fellow-travellers, whom Larry Ince had already introduced to their host. When Ince introduced Stone and Wade to him, the buffalo hunter finished by saying, "So, now you know who we are. May we, in turn, know who you are?"

"Certainly, Mr Ince," said the ghost town's sole resident. "My name is Ray Ablett, and I am the proprietor of this establishment."

Stone glanced round the deserted saloon, lit by only a couple of the overhead brass kerosene lamps. There was a pot-bellied stove standing near the bar, with its highly polished mahogany bar-top. To benefit from the heat emanating from the stove, one had to be within a few feet of it. The railed walkway running round the upper level of the saloon lay in darkness, while the bar-room itself was none too brightly illuminated. A scattering of tables and chairs indicated that once the saloon had catered for a host of miners, prospectors, gamblers and drinkers. Now it catered for nobody other than its proprietor. Stone observed a piano stuck away in one corner. So, there had even been music once.

"Wa'al," he drawled, "I guess I could do with a drink. What about you boys?" he asked, turning to the two buffalo hunters.

They both nodded their agreement.

"Whiskey for me," growled Jim Wade.

"An' for me," said Larry Ince eagerly.

"Miss Sally?" enquired Stone.

"I'd prefer some coffee, if 'n' you've got any?" she said, glancing from the Kentuckian to Ray Ablett.

"Yup. In the kitchen. You'll need to brew it yoreself," said Ablett, adding, "an' while yo're at it, there's some buttermilk in the pantry. Mebbe you can pour a glass for the li'l gal?"

Stone smiled. Some saloonkeepers barred Indians from their premises, refusing to serve them. He was relieved that Ablett was not among their number. He turned to Sally.

"That okay with you, Miss Sally?" he asked. "Will you take Grey Dove with you to the kitchen an' look after her?"

"'Course I will," replied Sally. She smiled warmly at the little Paiute. She was herself an orphan and she could sympathise with the girl over the loss of her parents and family. Besides, Grey Dove was such a pretty little thing that the blonde could not help but feel maternal towards her. One thing bothered her, though. "That lance," she said. "Why does she carry it?"

"It belonged to Grey Dove's father," explained Stone. "She ain't likely to easily relinquish it."

"Oh, wa'al, I don't s'pose it matters." Sally held out her hand to the Indian girl. "You come along with me, honey," she murmured.

92

Grey Dove looked mystified and not a little apprehensive. She glanced anxiously at the Kentuckian.

"It is all right," Stone assured her in the Paiute tongue. "The woman means you no harm. Go with her and she will give you some buttermilk."

Nervously, Grey Dove took hold of the blonde's hand.

"That's right, honey," said Sally. "You an' me, we'll be great pals."

The pair walked slowly across the bar-room towards the door which opened onto the narrow passage leading to the kitchen. Stone went with them and held open the door for them. As they passed through, Sally whispered imploringly, You gotta git me free of them buffalo hunters, Mr Stone."

"I'll see what I can do," Stone whispered back, though he felt he had his hands full looking after Grey Dove, without tackling the likes of Jim Wade and Larry Ince.

By the time Stone returned to the bar-counter, Ray Ablett had poured out four glasses of whiskey, and he and the buffalo hunters were happily sipping theirs. Stone raised his glass and toasted the saloonkeeper.

"Yore health, Mr Ablett," he said.

"An' yore's, Mr Stone." Ablett eyed the Kentuckian curiously and said, "Tell me, how come you got that li'l Injun gal in tow?"

"I came across her village some miles south of here, in Duck Valley. Entire Paiute band had been wiped out, massacred," said Stone.

"By whom?"

"By the US Army."

"They must've had a reason."

"Oh, they did! They're the kinda bastards who enjoy rapin' women an' murderin' children. That's the way they git their fun."

"All soldiers ain't like that, Mr Stone."

"Nope, I guess not. Anyways, I'm takin' Grey Dove to her grandpa on the Paiute reservation up north at Battle Mountain."

"I see." Ablett turned to the buffalo hunters and said, "An' the woman, she's some beauty. What's she doin' here?"

"We won her in a poker game," said Larry Ince.

"Jeeze! Who in hell would stake her in a poker game, or any other kinda game for that matter?" demanded Ablett incredulously.

"A gamblin' man, name of Pete Sangster," said Jim Wade.

"There's certainly some strange folks about."

"Wa'al, you ain't exactly conformin' yoreself," said Stone. "Surely it's a mite eccentric to be runnin' a saloon in a ghost town?"

Ray Ablett laughed and tugged at his moustache. He pointed towards the piano in one corner of the saloon.

"That's mine," he said. "I was the piano player in the Ace of Hearts Saloon in Carson City, 'bout three years back. Won me a whole stack of money on the roulette wheel, enough to come out to Silver Seam an' build this here saloon. Silver Seam was a boom town then, an' I had three good years 'fore the seam ran out. That was last December, an' everyone had up an' left by New Year's Day. Whole goddam town jest died."

"But you stayed on," said Stone.

"Yup. I had sufficient provisions to see me through the winter, so I reckoned I might as well stay put until the spring. Besides my reg'lar stores, I had a cow, two pigs an' several chickens. They're out back," explained Ablett.

"Yeah. We saw 'em, but I counted only one pig," said the Kentuckian.

"That's 'cause I slaughtered the other one. Been eatin' it ever since." Ablett grinned and continued, "I figure on movin' out any day now an' headin' back to Carson City. I aim to sell off all the bar-stock an' other provisions an' also the livestock. Then, with what I git an' what I've accumulated in the three years I've been here, I hope to buy me a share in one of the city's saloons."

"An' if there ain't nobody willin' to take you on as a pardner, what then?" enquired Stone.

"Wa'al, guess I'll jest have to go back to piano-playin'," said Ablett.

Stone grinned.

"You ain't proposin' to sell the piano, then?" he said.

"Hell no! That stays with me. Any saloon-keeper'll tell you that music is good for business. So, even if none of Carson City's saloonkeepers wants me for a pardner, you can bet yore bottom dollar one or other of 'em'll take me on as a piano player."

"Wa'al, I wish you luck." Stone drained his glass and, replacing it on the mahogany counter, he said, "Same again, an' this time one of these fellers is payin'."

The two buffalo hunters glanced at each other, but they didn't argue. Jim Wade paid for a fresh round of drinks out of the money he had won back in Clinton Falls.

Outside, the snow had been falling faster by the minute and the wind was whipping it in, both over and under the batwing doors, to form a drift just inside the bar-room. The blizzard showed no signs of abating. Indeed, Stone reckoned it was set to continue full-pelt throughout the night.

While he and his companions kept the cold at bay by clustering round the pot-bellied stove and drinking red-eye, Sally McBride and Grey Dove were in the kitchen, crouched beside the fire while they waited for the coffee to brew. Grey Dove had propped her father's lance against the kitchen table and was sitting on a low stool, sipping buttermilk. She watched as Sally poured herself a cup of coffee. Their eyes met and they smiled shyly. Although Sally knew no Paiute and Grey Dove knew no English, they both instinctively liked each other and, what was more important, Grey Dove felt she could trust the blondehaired white woman. After her horrific experience with Captain George Riley and his troop of US Cavalry, she had soon encountered two white people whom she respected and did not fear, Sally and the Kentuckian gunfighter, Jack Stone. Following the murder of her family, the girl might easily have come to regard all white people with the fear and loathing she felt for Riley and his men. However, her father's dying words had weighed heavily with her, and she recognised that all were not as vicious and depraved as the horse soldiers who had ridden into Duck Valley.

Nonetheless, she remained nervous and wary, for the situation in which she found herself was strange to her. And when, suddenly, she saw a face at the kitchen window, she immediately let out a yell, grabbed hold of the lance and crouched down facing the door. There was terror in her eyes and the lance was held at the ready, pointing in the direction of the door.

Slowly, the door opened, and a snow-covered figure staggered inside. He slammed the door shut and promptly began to shake himself free of the snow.

"Goddamn it, but it's hell out there!" gasped Pete Sangster.

"What in tarnation are you doin' here, Pete?" demanded Sally, staring incredulously at the gambler.

"I came after you. Been trackin' you all the way from Clinton Falls," said Sangster.

Sally turned to Grey Dove.

"It's okay, honey," she said, "you can put up the lance. He's a friend."

Grey Dove might not have understood the blonde's exact words, but she gleaned their general meaning. Still, she was not entirely convinced. She abandoned her defensive crouch and went and sat again on the low stool beside the fire, but she did not relinquish her hold of the lance.

"I'm 'bout frozen," confessed the gambler.

"I ain't surprised," said Sally, eyeing him closely and observing he was wearing no top-coat. "Here, sit by the fire an' git this cup of coffee down you," she added, handing him the cup she had just poured for herself.

While she poured herself another cup, she asked, "So, what's the plan? You really come to take me away from those goddam buffalo hunters?"

"That's 'bout it, Sal. I sold the buggy an' saddled both mares. They're stabled further down the street, outa sight of the saloon. So, jest as soon as this blizzard lets up, you an' me, we'll lam outa this ghost town an' be miles away 'fore them two fellers even realise yo're gone."

"An' in the meantime?"

"You string 'em along. Don't do nuthin' to antagonise 'em. We want 'em totally relaxed an' off their guard." Sangster glanced towards the kitchen's interior door. "They ain't likely to come along here, are they?" he asked anxiously.

"I shouldn't think so. The proprietor might, though."

"Hmm. That could prove awkward."

"He seems a decent 'nough kinda feller. You explain things to him, I don't think he'll split on you."

Sangster nodded and then pointed at Grey Dove.

"But what about the li'l Injun gal? Can we rely on her to keep her mouth shut?" he demanded.

Sally laughed.

"You ain't got no fears there," she said. "Grey Dove don't speak no English. Ain't that right, Grey Dove?" she added, smiling at the Paiute.

Grey Dove smiled back, but still did not relinquish her grip on the lance. She did not entirely trust the darkly handsome gambler in his expensive, city-style suit, which only went to prove that she was a much better judge of character than the blonde.

5

ROSCOE CUTTER and Billy Jackson had ridden hard and fast, and had put a good few miles between themselves and Barton's Ford before eventually, as dusk began to fall, finding a spot to camp for the night.

Supper had comprised of buck rabbit, some hard tack and a jug of freshly brewed coffee. The two robbers had eaten well enough, but neither man slept well. Both feared pursuit and, consequently, stirred at the slightest sound. Also, Billy Jackson's arm wound continued to pain him. Therefore, dawn came as a blessed relief, and the two cousins quickly rose and prepared to break camp. A couple of cups of coffee sufficed for breakfast and, in next to no time, they were ready to hit the trail again.

They had not gone more than a couple of miles, however, when Billy Jackson began to complain about his wound. His cousin glanced anxiously over his shoulder and growled, "Hell, Billy, we gotta press on, for we don't want no posse to catch up with us! If 'n' we git ourselves caught, we're gonna hang for sure."

The younger man's face was chalk-white, and the pain from his wound showed in his eyes, giving them a tense, strained look. It was clear that he was incapable of continuing the ride for much longer, without some form of medical attention. Cutter scowled, but, nevertheless, pulled up his sorrel. He turned to face Billy Jackson.

"Okay," he said, "let's take a look at yore goddam arm."

The two men dismounted and led their horses into the shelter of a nearby hollow. Situated at the foot of a low hill, it protected them from the bitter wind. For this, at least, both were duly grateful.

Jackson removed his sheepskin coat and displayed his wounded arm, which was held in a sling. Cutter had earlier made this from the tail of his cousin's spare shirt. It, like the one Jackson was wearing, was of a bright yellow and brown check, though the sling was, by now, soaked in blood.

Cutter gingerly removed the sling and the rough bandages, which had been torn from the remainder of Jackson's spare shirt. He was as careful as he could be, yet still Jackson cried out in agony. Cutter did not like what he saw. The flesh around the wound had turned black. Unless he was much mistaken, it was gangrenous. He forced a weak smile.

"It ain't so bad, Billy," he lied.

"No?" gasped Jackson.

"No. Soon as we hit town, we'll pay the doc a visit an' he'll fix you up as good as new."

"An' what town are we aimin' to hit?"

"I ain't rightly sure, but we seem to

be headin' in the general direction of Imlay."

Wa'al, I hope we git there soon, for my arm don't feel none to good. I guess mebbe it's infected?"

"Naw, it's jest hurtin' 'cause it's a recent wound. You said you reckoned the slug had broke the bone. So, it figures it's gonna pain you for a while."

Cutter spoke confidently, trying to convince his cousin that there was nothing to worry about. Privately, he reckoned that Billy Jackson would be lucky if all he lost was he left arm. He hastily tore some fresh shreds from what little remained of the spare shirt, and re-bandaged the wound. Then, he helped Jackson place his arm back into the bloodstained sling, which he proceeded to fasten round his cousin's neck. This done, he hoisted Jackson up onto the saddle of his tan gelding.

"Now, let's lam outa here," he rasped, as he swiftly mounted the sorrel.

The two gunslingers trotted slowly out of the hollow and began to canter up the side of the low hill. As they did so, the wind cut into their faces, forcing them to screw up their eyes. Consequently, when they breasted the brow of the hill, they were concentrating their gaze upon the necks of their horses, rather than upon the trail ahead. And, so, the lone rider loomed up in front of them as though he had sprouted from the very ground.

Billy Jackson was the first to recoguise the rider as none other than the young, fairhaired sheriff, who had chased them out of Barton's Ford and broken his, Jackson's arm with one of his parting shots. The bank robber promptly went for his gun. But, before the Remington had even cleared leather, Daniel Budge's Colt Peacemaker barked twice. The first shot struck Jackson in the chest, shattering his rib-cage and puncturing one lung. The second went clean through his open mouth and out through the back of his skull. And the force of the two shots knocked him from his saddle. He hit the ground with a dull thud and lay quite still.

Roscoe Cutter's reactions had been altogether slower than his cousin's, and his hand had barely come to rest upon the butt of his revolver by the time Billy Jackson was lying dead on the snow-covered trail and Daniel Budge was addressing him in a cold, harsh tone.

"You try drawin' that there Remington an' I'll plug you for sure," rasped the sheriff.

Cutter stared into the barrel of Budge's Colt Peacemaker and slowly withdrew his hand from the butt of his revolver. He raised both hands.

"I surrender," he said.

Budge smiled bleakly and glanced down at the lifeless body of Billy Jackson.

"It was hardly worth yore time

tendin' to his wound," he commented.

Cutter shrugged his shoulders.

"You been watchin' us?" he asked.

"Sure. I tracked you all the way from Barton's Ford. It was easy followin' yore tracks in the snow. Anyways, I figured you'd head north for Oregon." Budge smiled bleakly a second time and added, "I finally caught up with you a mile back. Been observin' you ever since."

"So, what now?"

"I aim on takin' you back to Barton's Ford for trial."

"For bank robbery?"

"For murder."

"But it was Billy there who shot the bank manager an' the woman. I never wanted nobody to git hurt."

Cutter knew that, should he be brought to trial, his only hope of escaping the noose would be by convincing the jury that this was the case. He prayed, therefore, that the bank clerk had not seen him fire the fatal shot at his boss. And he determined to protest his innocence all the way back to Barton's Ford, assuming, of course, that he did not succeed in escaping from the young sheriff before then.

"I had hoped to take you both in," said Budge, "for I was lookin' forward to seein' the pair of you dancin' at the end of a rope. Yore pardner, he got off too darned lightly."

"Aw, c'mon, Sheriff, ain't you takin' this a mite too personally?" said Cutter.

"Am I? Wa'al, mebbe that's 'cause the woman you gunned down happened to be my wife an' the mother of my two kids."

Although Budge spoke softly, there was a menacing note to his voice that Cutter could not fail to observe. He stared into the young sheriff's pale blue eyes and was met with a look of pure, unadulterated hatred.

"Hell, Sheriff, I wouldn't've shot yore wife! I wouldn't shoot no woman!" protested the gunman.

"It don't matter to me which of

you shot Laura," replied Budge coldly. "As far as I'm concerned, yo're both equally guilty. So, don't go givin' me no excuse to plug you, for, I tell you, I'm sorely tempted. Only the thought of you hangin', an' of the sweatin' yo're gonna do while yo're awaitin' trial, keeps me from fillin' you full of holes here an' now."

Cutter nodded nervously. He realised that Budge was itching to squeeze the trigger of his Colt Peacemaker, and he had no wish to die yet awhile. The thought of swinging from a gallows made his flesh creep, but he reckoned that a lot could happen before they returned to Barton's Ford. While he remained alive, there was always the chance that he might elude the noose.

"I . . . I ain't lookin' to 'cause you no problems, Sheriff. You'll find me a model prisoner," he promised.

Budge smiled grimly and produced a pair of handcuffs.

"Lower yore hands an' ride forward till we're abreast of each other," he said. "But don't try nuthin', or I'll shoot you dead."

Cutter eyed the Colt pointing directly at his heart and decided to do exactly as the sheriiff had bidden him. He edged forward, gently prodding the sorrel's flanks with the heels of his unspurred boots. The animal responded and quietly stepped up alongside the sheriff's roan. Immediately, Budge barked out an order.

"Hands together. Now stretch 'em out towards me!"

"Like this?" enquired Cutter, and he held out both hands straight in front of him.

"That's right," said Budge, and he swiftly handcuffed the gunslinger's wrists together.

This accomplished, Budge proceeded to disarm the outlaw. He pulled the Winchester from the saddleboot and the Remington from Cutter's holster, and tossed both into the snow. Then he motioned with his Colt Peacemaker that the outlaw should head back down the trail in the direction from which he had come.

"What about Billy?" asked Cutter.

"What about Billy?" demanded Budge irritably.

"Surely he's entitled to a Christian burial?"

"We ain't got no shovels to dig no grave."

"We could take him back to Barton's Ford an . . ."

"We could, but we won't."

"But, if 'n' we don't, he'll be picked to pieces by buzzards, or coyotes, or . . ."

"A fittin' end for the murderin' sonofabitch. Food for coyotes is all he's good for." Budge scowled and prodded Cutter hard in the ribs with his Colt. "Now git movin'!" he snapped.

Cutter made no further protest. He turned the sorrel's head and set off down the trail. Budge followed a pace or two behind the sorrel, leading Billy Jackson's gelding on a long rein. He slipped the revolver back into its holster and removed the Winchester from the saddleboot. With the rifle resting easily in the crook of his arm, he felt confident he would not lose his prisoner. Should Cutter make a sudden dash for freedom, there was no way he would get beyond the range of the rifle before Budge drew a bead on him and squeezed the trigger.

They rode in silence. Budge was lost in thoughts of his dead wife and motherless children, while Cutter was feverishly racking his brains for some means of escape. The hours passed and the sky grew progressively darker, as ominous black clouds built up overhead. By mid-day, it was obvious to both men that a storm was brewing. It was Cutter, though, who first mentioned the fact.

"Sheriff," he said, "don't you think we should find ourselves some place to rest up? There's a storm comin', an' we don't wanta git caught out in it, do we?"

Budge said nothing, although in fact he agreed with the outlaw. He feared that Cutter might take advantage of the storm to give him the slip. As the snow began to fall, he took his lariat from his saddlebow and neatly lassoed the gunslinger, a trick he had learned in his cowpunching days, before he became a lawman.

"What in tarnation are you doin'?" exclaimed Cutter.

"Jest makin' sure I don't lose you," replied Budge quietly.

Cutter swore roundly. He had hoped the snowstorm might provide him with an opportunity to escape.

The snow, driven by the fierce March wind, began to fall faster and faster. Soon a full-scale blizzard was raging and neither rider could see more than a few yards ahead of him. Fearing that should they halt out there in the open, they might' freeze to death, Daniel Budge kept them moving. He peered to his left and to his right in search of somewhere to shelter, but the density of the falling snowflakes was such that he could observe little or nothing. Therefore, he continued blindly on down the trail, hoping that he would not stray from it.

In fact, the trail had forked a mile or two back from where Budge had finally caught up with the two bank robbers. And, upon approaching this fork in the midst of the blizzard, the two riders inadvertently took the trail that led away from Barton's Ford. A further mile's ride found them descending into a wide valley. The trail was, by now, almost completely obliterated, and Budge wondered whether they had lost it altogether. At this point, he was interrupted by an excited yell from his prisoner.

"Hey, Sheriff, here's some kinda signpost!"

Budge rode up alongside the outlaw, half-suspecting a trick. But Cutter had spoken the truth. Budge hurriedly brushed the snow from the signpost and read the following legend: "Silver Seam ½ mile."

"Look's like we're gonna make it," he said.

They urged their horses into a trot, and soon found themselves riding into the one-time mining town and along its deserted street.

"Jeeze, it's a goddam ghost town!" exclaimed Cutter.

"Wa'al, it ain't entirely deserted," responded Budge. "Look, there's light spillin' out onto the sidewalk up ahead."

Cutter peered through the falling snow and saw a small stretch of street and sidewalk illuminated by the dim light from Ray Ablett's kerosene lamps.

They rode up to the Silver Dollar Saloon and Daniel Budge swiftly dismounted. He prodded Cutter with the barrel of his Winchester.

"Okay, git down, an' don't try no tricks," he rasped.

Cutter smiled wryly. What kind of tricks did the sheriff expect him to try?

He was disarmed, handcuffed and had the lawman's lariat pulled tight round his shoulders.

The two men slowly climbed up onto the stoop and entered the saloon through the batwing doors. Their entry caused the three drinkers at the bar to turn round, while the saloonkeeper, who had been busily feeding the pot-bellied stove with wood, straightened up, grinned broadly and addressed them in a jovial voice.

"Howdy, fellers. Welcome to the Silver Dollar, the finest establishment of its kind in Tumbleweed City, indeed the only establishment of any kind still open in Tumbleweed City."

"Yeah, I had noticed," said Budge. "How come yo're still open, when the town's dead as mutton."

Ray Ablett tugged at his moustache and then proceeded to give the sheriff the same explanation that he had earlier given Stone and the others.

When the saloonkeeper had finshed, Stone removed the cheroot from his mouth and drawled, "What about you, stranger? How come you've got that feller all roped up an' are holdin' a gun on him?"

"'Cause he's wanted for bank robbery an' murder." Budge pulled open his sheepskin coat to reveal the tin star clipped to his vest pocket. "Sheriff Daniel Budge of Barton's Ford. An' this here's the murderin' bastard who robbed the bank there an' gunned down two innocent people, one of whom was my wife."

Budge spat out these words while regarding Cutter with the kind of venomous stare that a man usually reserves for rattlesnakes and other such vermin.

"I tell you, Sheriff, I didn't shoot nobody!" protested Cutter.

"He had a pardner," said Budge. "Claims he did the shootin'."

"But you don't believe him," said Stone.

"Nope."

"You say, Sheriff, that he an' his

119

pardner robbed a bank?" said Larry Ince.

"That's right."

"The pardner, where is he?" enquired Ince.

"I shot him back along the trail."

"An' the money they're s'posed to have taken from this bank in Barton's Ford, whereabouts is it?" asked Jim Wade.

Daniel Budge eyed the four men warily. There was a lot of money stached in the saddlebags which were draped over Roscoe Cutter's sorrel and Billy Jackson's gelding. Enough to tempt a man to theft, maybe even murder. The saloonkeeper looked harmless enough, but the other three struck Budge as pretty rough, tough customers.

"'Fore I say anythin' more, hows 'bout introducin' yoreselves?" he said.

"Fair enough," replied Stone. "My name's Jack Stone an' I'm . . . "

"Jack Stone!" ejaculated the young sheriff, and a relieved smile split his youthful features. "I've heard of you, Mr Stone. Why, yo're one of the most famous lawmen in the entire West. Reckon I can trust you all right."

"That you can, Sheriff, though I ain't a lawman no more. These days, I'm more concerned with avoidin' trouble than confrontin' it," said the Kentuckian.

Stone's presence reassured Daniel Budge. He reckoned that, with Stone as an ally, he had nothing to fear from the others. He listened while Larry Ince and Jim Wade introduced themselves and explained that they were buffalo hunters on their way north to Oregon. Ray Ablett had already explained his presence in Silver Seam, and now he gave the sheriff his name and offered him a whiskey.

"Thanks, Mr Ablett, but I guess I'll see to the hosses first," said Budge.

"What about the money? You was gonna tell us 'bout the money," said Ince.

"Was I?"

"It's in our saddlebags outside," interjected Roscoe Cutter.

"Is that so?" muttered Larry Ince.

Budge glared at the bank robber. He had been about to tell the buffalo hunter that Cutter and his cousin had failed in their attempt to rob the bank and leave it at that, hoping that Larry Ince and Jim Wade would assume no money had been taken. Now they knew otherwise, and he would have to be on his guard, for he had noted the avaricious gleam that appeared in, and then quickly vanished from, both the buffalo hunters' eyes.

"Sit down," he snarled, pushing Cutter towards a chair at a nearby poker table.

Budge produced a key from his vest pocket and unfastened one of the handcuffs. Then, he snapped this shut round one of the legs of the poker table. Smiling grimly, he thereupon proceeded to bind the bank robber to the chair, using the length of rope with which he had earlier lassoed him. And, when eventually Cutter was trussed up like a Thanksgiving turkey, he stepped back and admired his handiwork.

"Don't reckon you'll be goin' anywheres for a li'l while," he said confidently. Then, turning to the saloonkeeper, he enquired, "Is there some place I can stable the hosses?"

"There's stables round the back of the saloon," replied Ablett.

"I'll give you a hand," offered Stone, stubbing out his cheroot and throwing back the remains of his whiskey.

"Gee, thanks, Mr Stone! I'd sure 'preciate that," said the sheriff gratefully.

The stabling of the three horses took a little while and, this time, Stone did not suggest they return through the kitchen. Sally McBride and Grey Dove had offered to fix supper and he had no wish to disturb them. Therefore, he and the sheriff slipped back up the alleyway between the saloon and the one-time barbering parlour, and re-entered the bar-room through the batwing doors at the front.

They each carried a pair of the saddlebags belonging to the two bank robbers. The sheriff also carried his Winchester. They propped the saddlebags against the piano in the corner of the bar-room, and Budge placed a chair directly in front of it. He laid the Winchester across the chair and joined the others at the bar, where he proceeded to order a fresh round of drinks.

"Okay, fellers," he said to the buffalo hunters. "That's where I aim to stay till this here blizzard blows itself out. So, if 'n' you have any idea of grabbin' the money in them saddlebags, I should forget it."

Jim Wade shrugged his broad shoulders and grinned.

"The thought never crossed our minds; did it, Larry?" he growled.

"Never," affirmed his partner.

At this point, the interior door was pushed open, and Sally and Grey Dove appeared, bearing plates of food. The little Paiute had helped Sally prepare the meal and, despite the lack of a common tongue, they had become firm friends. Sally's only worry was that Grey Dove might confide in Stone regarding the presence of Pete Sangster in the kitchen. It was not that she minded the Kentuckian knowing. It was just that she was afraid he might, in turn, let the information slip to the two buffalo hunters.

In the event, Grey Dove said little to the Kentuckian, and he made no comment about Pete Sangster's presence in the kitchen. Sally's hopes began to rise again. She prayed that the blizzard would peter out during the night, so that she and Sangster could be well on their way before Larry Ince and Jim Wade awoke. Sally was no horsewoman, yet she reckoned that she and the gambler on horseback should easily out-distance the buffalo hunters with their wagon and mules. She smiled to herself. In those circumstances, they would almost certainly give her up as a lost cause and continue on their journey to Oregon.

The meal consisted of rye bread, pork and beans, and coffee, and was much appreciated by the hungry travellers. Sally and Grey Dove sat with Jack Stone, the saloonkeeper and the two buffalo hunters at one table, while Daniel Budge and Roscoe Cutter dined at another. Despite Cutter's pleading, the sheriff refused to release the outlaw from either the handcuffs or the rope binding him to the chair. In consequence, Cutter had some difficulty in eating the meal, having only limited freedom with his left hand. Hunger was a sharp spur, however, and he managed.

When the meal was eaten and another round of coffee poured, Daniel Budge retired to the chair in front of the piano. He placed the Winchester across his knees and viewed the others with a fairly relaxed eye. He felt secure in the knowledge that the bank's money was stashed safely away behind him, and that the surviving bank robber was bound hand and foot and handcuffed to the poker table.

An equally relaxed Jack Stone lit a cheroot and, smiling across at Sally, said, "Compliments to the cook, Miss Sally. That was as tasty a meal as I've eaten in many a long month."

"Thank you, Mr Stone. Guess you was a li'l surprised I could cook, huh?" replied Sally, with a smile.

The Kentuckian grinned.

"Wa'al, it ain't a talent a man gen'rally expects to find in a sportin' woman," he confessed.

6

THE blizzard raged on through the night and showed no sign of relenting. Eventually, as the midnight hour approached, it was decided that they should all turn in for the night. Grey Dove had retired some hours earlier and Sally proposed to share her bed, but this brought protests from the two buffalo hunters, both of whom had had several whiskies and were feeling more than a little randy.

"Hell no!" exclaimed Jim Wade. "You gonna share anybody's bed, it's gotta be mine or Larry's."

"That's right, Miss Sally; we won you fair 'n' square in that poker game. So, now yo're ours to do with as we please, an' it pleases us to have you share our bed," added Lary Ince.

"Share your bed? Are you proposin'

we sleep three in a bed?" cried the blonde.

"Yeah. Why not? Me an' Larry, we share everythin' else. Why shouldn't we share the same woman in the same bed?" growled Wade.

Sally had already spent one night satisfying the gross sexual appetites of the two buffalo hunters, and she had no wish to spend another such night. At least in the back of the wagon she had been able to roll free of them once their needs were filled. Trapped between the pair in one bed, she would be stuck for the entire night, which would make things more than a little difficult if the storm abated and she wanted to slip away to the kitchen and make her escape with Pete Sangster.

"Once we git back on the trail, I guess you fellers can call the tune," she said. "But, for tonight, I figure on havin' me some privacy."

"What about the Injun gal? She . . . " began Ince.

"Is sound asleep. She won't bother

129

me none," retorted Sally.

"Wa'al, I'm tellin' you that yo're goin' to bed with us," rasped Wade.

"I don't think so," intervened Stone. He eyed the two buffalo hunters coldly and said, "I ain't sure 'bout the legality of winnin' a woman at poker, partickerly when the feller you won her off wasn't even her husband."

"Now listen here . . . " began Wade.

"No, you boys listen. As I said, I ain't sure 'bout the legality, but then I ain't no lawyer. So, I won't make it an issue." Stone wanted to make it an issue, wanted to free the woman, but he had enough on his hands escorting Grey Dove to the reservation at Battle Mountain, without involving himself in a gun-fight with the buffalo hunters. Although he figured he could take them, he had no real inclination to do so. After all, the bet had been made by Sally's lover and the conditions had been agreed to by her. "All I'm sayin', boys, is that, while yo're under this roof, you should respect Miss Sally's wishes. What you do once you git back on the trail is yore business."

"I agree," said Ray Ablett. "You got her to do with as you like all the way to Oregon."

"If 'n' she don't run off!" exclaimed Ince.

"Wa'al, you'll have to see that she don't. Anyways, surely you can let her have one last night to herself?" The saloonkeeper spoke quietly, a conciliatory smile on his face, and, as he spoke, he poured the buffalo hunters another couple of drinks. "On the house," he said genially.

"Wa'al . . . " began Wade.

"I think you'd best concede, fellers," stated Daniel Budge, from his seat in the corner.

The sheriff, like Stone, was none too happy about the bet. Unfortunately, again like Stone, he felt his hands were tied, for his duty was clear. It was to bring Roscoe Cutter to trial and return the saddlebags full of money to the Cattlemen's Bank in Barton's

Ford. Therefore, he dared not risk a confrontation with Wade and Ince.

The buffalo hunters exchanged glances, then Wade shrugged his brawny shoulders and Ince spoke.

"Okay," he said reluctantly. "You win. Miss Sally can spend tonight with the Injun gal. But, tomorrow, once the storm's over, she comes with us. Right?"

"Right," said Ablett.

Stone nodded and Budge indicated his agreement with a casual wave of his hand.

"Thank you," said the blonde.

Relieved, Sally quickly got to her feet and bade them all a hasty good-night. Then she hurried from the bar-room. But she did not make her way directly to the bedroom in which Grey Dove was sleeping. Instead, she headed for the firelit kitchen, where she found Pete Sangster slumped in an armchair before the fire. He promptly rose and pulled her into his arms.

When, eventually, they had finished

kissing, she whispered, "It's okay. I'm sleepin' in the first bedroom you come to on yore left. As soon as the snow stops, come an' git me."

"You sleepin' alone?" enquired Sangster.

"That li'l Injun gal is there with me. But she won't betray us," said Sally.

"I sure hope not."

"No. Anyways, I'd best be goin'."

"Why not stay here with me? It's warm 'n' cosy an' . . . "

"S'pose one of them buffalo hunters comes along to check I'm where I'm s'posed to be?"

"Why in tarnation would he?"

"'Cause they both know I'm liable to run out on 'em. I tried it a coupla times on the trail an' they ended up ropin' me to their wagon."

"Holy cow!"

"You got me into one helluva mess, Pete!"

"I know, Sal. But, don't worry, we'll be hightailin' it outa here in a few hours. Jest as soon as that there storm abates."

"Okay." The blonde clasped her arms round the back of Sangster's neck and, pressing her soft, warm body against his, kissed him passionately on the lips. Then, before he could stop her, she pulled herself free and stepped across to the door leading to the corridor. "Come as soon as you can," she said softly, and was gone.

The sleeping arrangements for the others were simple. Jim Wade and Larry Ince were not, after all, to share a bed. They were each to have a bedroom upstairs, as was Jack Stone. The rooms had been used by the saloon girls in the Silver Dollar's heyday, and each contained a much-used single bed. Ray Ablett had his own bedroom downstairs, opposite that occupied by Sally McBride and Grey Dove. As for Sheriff Daniel Budge, he remained in his chair in the corner of the bar-room, while his prisoner was due to spend an uncomfortable night tied up and and handcuffed to the poker table.

Only Grey Dove and Ray Ablett slept well that night. Upon retiring, Grey Dove's thoughts had returned to Duck Valley and the massacre of her family. But sheer exhaustion had finally overtaken her and she had cried herself to sleep.

Ray Ablett, on the other hand, had begun to snore immediately his head hit the pillow.

The others were much too keyed up to fall asleep so easily.

Stone still wondered whether to intervene between the blonde and the buffalo hunters. His promise to Two Elks inclined him to steer clear of that particular problem, as did his natural inclination to avoid trouble wherever possible. Yet he felt truly sorry for the girl, and his conscience told him that he should not let them cart her off against her will. He was still debating the matter when he drifted off into an uneasy sleep.

Both Sally McBride and Pete

Sangster remained wide awake for some considerable time.

The girl eagerly anticipated the end of the blizzard and her escape from Silver Seam, while the gambler struggled manfully with his fatigue, anxious to spot the moment the snow stopped and act upon it. In the event, both eventually dropped into a doze.

Daniel Budge had the same trouble as Pete Sangster. He was determined to remain awake, fearful lest Cutter should, by some means or other, engineer an escape. Common sense told him this was not possible, yet still Budge struggled to keep his eyes open. But he had had an exhausting day, and the combined effects of a good meal and several whiskies were beginning to tell on him. He gradually grew drowsier and drowsier, and, around three o'clock in the morning, he finally succumbed. His head dropped forward onto his chest and he fell fast asleep. His prisoner, however, did no such thing. Rosco Cutter remained wide awake.

Upstairs, the two buffalo hunters had passed a fitful night dozing, then waking, then dozing again. It was four o'clock, or a few minutes past, when Larry Ince entered his partner's room and shook him awake.

"Wha . . . what is it?" gasped Jim Wade.

"Ssh! Keep yore goddam voice down," hissed Ince.

"Wa'al, whaddya mean by wakin' me up like that?" retorted Wade in a gruff whisper.

"It's stopped snowin'," was the other's response.

"So?"

"So, mebbe we should discuss the situation."

"What are you talkin' about? What's there to discuss?" enquired Wade.

Ince pulled on his beard and replied, "That there woman. S'pose Stone or the sheriff, or both of 'em, take it into their heads to set her free?"

"They won't do that. They've said as much. They have both got enough

137

on their minds without tanglin' with us."

"Mebbe? Mebbe not?"

"So, what are yuh sayin, Larry? That we should abandon her?"

"There's plenty of pretty women in places like Reno, or Dodge, or Abilene, or . . . "

"Sure there is. Only we ain't headin' for any of them places. We're headin' out into the wilds of Oregon."

"Are we?"

"Sure we are, Larry. We're goin' there to hunt buffalo like we've always done."

"They ain't so easy to find these days."

"Nope. But it's the only trade we know."

"We got us some gamblin' winnin's. We could change our plans an' head, instead, for Reno or Carson City."

"Aw, c'mon, Larry! How long d'you reckon them winnin's'll last? But, with them an' what we git for the buffalo hides we collect this summer, we could take some time out, sure. First, though we gotta . . ."

"I know where we can git more money 'n we'll ever git from huntin' buffalo."

Jim Wade stared round-eyed at his companion. He was wide awake now.

"Are you thinkin' what I figure yo're thinkin'?" he asked in a low growl.

"The money in them saddlebags."

"We don't know how much."

"Enough to keep us in whiskey an' women for a few months, if not years."

"You reckon?"

"Sure, Jim."

"Wa'al, I dunno."

"They're there for the takin'. We slip downstairs, slug that there sheriff, an' we're off 'fore you can say Jack."

"What about Stone? I don't fancy no confrontation with that sonofabitch."

"He's fast asleep. We'll be long gone 'fore he wakes up."

"I still don't like the idea of givin' up that blonde. Hell, she's one helluva beautiful woman!"

"Miss Sally McBride ain't the only beautiful woman in the West. An' with plenty of money in our pockets, we'll have women who ain't only beautiful, but are a darned sight more accomodatin'. For a sportin' woman, she ain't so goddam co-operative, now is she?"

"No. Mebbe not."

"Then, come on, git dressed, an' let's git goin'."

"Jest like that, huh? Have you thought 'bout the sheriff?"

"My guess is, he'll be sound asleep."

"An' if he ain't?"

"I'll plug him 'fore he knows what's what."

"That'll waken the whole household for sure."

"So? We'll be outa here, mounted an' away 'fore they've even got their pants on."

Jim Wade scowled. He was uncertain what to do. A huge mountain of a man, he was as rough and tough as any of his fellow buffalo hunters, and they were an extremely rough, tough breed of men. However, he had never before robbed anyone. Nor had he killed anyone, not unless you counted that half-breed he had beaten to death in a drunken brawl. But that, he reflected, had been a fair fight.

"Okay," he said, after some moments' consideration. "Let's go do it."

He dressed quickly and, a few minutes later, the two men were outside on the railed walkway, peering down into the semi-darkness of the saloon. They each clutched an unloaded buffalo gun in one hand and a loaded Colt revolver in the other. Wade favoured a Peacemaker, while Ince carried a Frontier Model. Slowly, cautiously, they descended the wooden staircase to the floor of the bar-room.

Then, they carefully picked their way through the tables and chairs towards the figure slumped in a chair, in the corner of the room where the piano stood. Ablett had doused the kerosene lamps upon retiring to bed, but there was enough of dawn's early light to enable them to see where they were going.

As they warily approached the piano, it became apparent that Larry Ince's guess was correct. Daniel Budge, exhausted and unable to keep his eyes open for a moment longer, had finally dropped off to sleep and now was submerged in a deep slumber.

Ince grinned wolfishly, then reversed his revolver and brought the butt crashing down on the young sheriff's unprotected skull. Budge grunted and slid off the chair to lie in a crumpled heap on the floor. His Winchester would have fallen, too, had not Wade, who had propped his buffalo gun against the bar, managed to catch it with his free hand. He laid the Winchester carefully down on a nearby table and retrieved the buffalo gun. Meanwhile, Ince crouched down beside the spreadeagled body of the sheriff.

"He's out for the count, but he's

still breathin'," Ince informed his giant companion.

"Then, you should've hit him harder," a voice advised him.

The two buffalo hunters whirled round and found themselves staring at Roscoe Cutter, who, although bound and handcuffed, was wide awake. He stared straight back at them and grinned.

"We . . . we thought you was asleep," growled Wade.

"Wa'al, you thought wrong. Trussed up like this, I ain't had hardly a wink of sleep all night." Cutter nodded towards the piano in the corner, against which Daniel Budge and the Kentuckian had propped his and Billy Jackson's saddlebags. "You fellers figurin' on makin' off with that money me an' Billy took from the Cattlemen's Bank in Barton's Ford?" he enquired.

"An' what if we are?"

"One yell from me will awaken the whole goddam household, an' that'll bring Stone runnin'. You reckon you can out-gun him?"

"We won't have to. We'll be outa here 'fore he's even got his pants on," said Ince.

"Don't bet on it. Stone ain't a man to worry 'bout niceties like dressin'. Not in an emergency. He'll come outa his bedroom stark naked, you mark my words. But he'll be carryin' his Frontier Model Colt, an' he'll gun you down 'fore you can make it to yore hosses."

The bank robber's words gave the buffalo hunters cause for thought. If he was right and Stone did not pause even to pull on his pants . . .

Larry Ince and Jim Wade exchanged worried glances. Both could handle a gun, but neither was a professional gunflghter, whereas Stone most certainly was. And Stone's reputation, like Bat Masterson's and Wild Bill Hickok's, was so awesome, it was sufficient to scare most men half to death. The buffalo hunters were no exception.

"Okay," said Ince. "So, whaddya want?"

"I want freein', an' I want one half of the bank haul. You two can split Billy's share between you."

"Oh, no!" said Ince. "We free you an' we split the money three ways, one third each."

"I agree," growled Wade.

Cutter, realising that time was of the essence, decided to argue no further. He wanted the money, but, more than anything, he wanted his freedom. The sooner he crossed the state line into Oregon and found sanctuary with his kin-folk the better.

"Okay, boys, you got a deal," he said. "Now, git me outa this. An', in case yo're wonderin', the key to these handcuffs is in the sheriff's vest pocket."

While Jim Wade was untying the bonds binding Cutter to the chair, Larry Ince bent down and fumbled in the sheriff's vest pocket. He removed the key and proceeded to unlock the handcuffs. Then, as he and Wade went over into the corner and picked up the two pairs of saddlebags, Roscoe Cutter slowly rose to his feet and began vigorously rubbing life back into his stiff limbs.

"Right, let's lam outa here," said Ince, throwing one of the two pairs of saddlebags over his left shoulder.

"Yeah, we've wasted enough time already," growled Wade, doing likewise with the other pair.

"Gimme a moment," retorted Cutter, and he crouched down beside the sheriff and pulled Daniel Budge's Colt Peacemaker from its holster. He straightened up. "Okay. Let's go," he said.

"The hosses are stabled out back, so we'll cut through the kitchen," stated Ince.

The three men hurried across the bar-room, and Ince quietly opened the door leading into the short, narrow corridor that ran between the two downstairs bedrooms to the kitchen. They tiptoed gingerly along the corridor, and Ince pushed open the kitchen door.

Although he did so with the utmost caution, the door creaked alarmingly as it swung back.

The noise was by no means enough to waken the dead. However, it was quite sufficient to waken Sangster from his light slumbers. He leapt to his feet and, upon observing the shadowy figures in the doorway, gasped, "Who the hell . . . "

But that was as far as he got, for Roscoe Cutter immediately reacted to the sight of the gambler all of a sudden looming into view. The outlaw aimed and fired Daniel Budge's Colt in one swift, instinctive movement. Fortunately for Sangster, the shot was hurried and went wide of its target.

Sangster dived for cover behind the kitchen table, at the same time drawing his pearl-handled British Tranter. He was no gunman, though, and his two responding shots both failed to hit any of the three confederates. Nevertheless, they did persuade the trio to turn tail and run back along the corridor, in the hope of making an unopposed exit through the bar-room.

This was a mistake, for, no sooner had they re-entered the bar-room than Jack Stone appeared upon the railed walkway above them. He had hastily pulled on his denim pants, and, in his right hand, he clutched his trusty Frontier Model Colt. The Kentuckian's first shot whipped Roscoe Cutter's hat from his head, while his second struck the giant Jim Wade in the shoulder, sending him crashing backwards into Larry Ince. A third shot ripped through Cutter's coat, grazing his ribs.

"Aw, hell!" cried the bank robber, and he turned again and, pushing the two buffalo hunters aside, headed once more for the kitchen. He preferred to shoot it out with the shadowy stranger rather than with Jack Stone.

The shooting had woken the other occupants of the Silver Dollar Saloon and, as the bank robber and his two companions scrambled back towards the kitchen, both bedroom doors were flung open and Sally McBride and Ray Ablett stuck their heads out. A shot from Larry Ince's Colt revolver lodged in the doorpost a mere inch from Ablett's head, and the saloonkeeper straightway leapt back into the bedroom and slammed the door shut. Sally let out a shriek and did likewise.

The three gunmen sprinted on down the corridor, Wade clutching his wounded shoulder and struggling to hold onto his pair of saddlebags. Cutter was the first into the kitchen. He went through the doorway in a crouching, weaving run, blasting away with his Colt Peacemaker as he ran. He sprayed the kitchen with a volley of shots, hoping to hit the partially-hidden gambler with one or other of them. In this he was lucky. His third shot ripped through the top of the kitchen table and buried itself in Pete Sangster's thigh.

Sangster's response was again wildly inaccurate, and, as he screamed and fell sideways with blood oozing from he leg wound, the gun slipped from his grasp.

Cutter and the two buffalo hunters hurtled past his prostrate form and threw open the kitchen door. Then, just before he stepped out into the yard, Cutter turned and aimed a final shot at the gambler. He fired from point-blank range, and the slug hit Sangster in the centre of his forehead. It blasted through his brain and erupted out of the back of his skull in a cloud of blood, brains and bone splinters. Cutter grinned and dived out through the open doorway.

"Okay, let's git saddled up!" cried Ince, as he and Wade joined the bank robber outside in the snow.

Although it had ceased to fall, the snow lay thick upon the ground, and the three men had some trouble ploughing their way through it to the stables. They threw open the doors and plunged inside.

"You fellers saddle the hosses. I'll keep Stone an' the others pinned down," said Wade.

He lay down his saddlebags and,

crouching just inside the stable doors, took careful aim with his revolver. The moment anyone poked his head out of the kitchen door, Wade proposed to plant a bullet in it. However, he found that he had trouble concentrating, for his wounded shoulder was giving him a great deal of pain.

In the event, Stone was not foolish enough to poke his head out. Instead, he remained inside the kitchen and waited. He was joined by Ray Ablett, armed with the shotgun which he had fetched from behind the bar-counter.

"What are we gonna do, Mr Stone?" enquired the saloonkeeper.

"Wait for 'em to make a break for it, an' then blast 'em outa the saddle," replied the Kentuckian tersely.

Behind them, Pete Sangster lay motionless upon the floor. He would never again either discard a card or throw a dice. His gambling days were over.

The wait was of only a few minutes' duration. Then, all at once, the stable doors were thrown wide open and the three riders came galloping out into the waiting dawn. In the lead was Jim Wade. He presented a huge target as he raced across the yard, unconsciously shielding his partner and the bank robber from the Kentuckian's and the saloonkeeper's fire. Stone's first shot struck Wade in the belly, while Ray Ablett's shot-gun blast almost cut him in two. The combination of the two shots knocked the buffalo hunter out of the saddle, and he was dead before he hit the snowbound earth.

His confederates took full advantage of Stone's and Ablett's preoccupation with Jim Wade. While they were engaged in gunning him down, Roscoe Cutter and Larry Ince were swift to make their escape. Riding hell-for-leather, they were out of range before Stone and the saloonkeeper could draw a bead on them. Stone did loose off a couple of shots after them, though more in hope than in the expectation of actually hitting them. Galloping through the snow, they quickly regained the trail and sped northwards, up out of the valley.

Ray Ablett glanced at the Kentuckian and pulled thoughtfully at his moustache.

"The goddam sonsofbitches have got clean away!" he growled.

"But I guess they've left half their loot behind," remarked the Kentuckian, and he pointed towards the rangy roan standing about fifty yards off in the snow. Draped across his back was a pair of saddlebags.

The roan was Sheriff Daniel Budge's mount and had been taken by Jim Wade. Roscoe Cutter had ridden his own horse, the sorrel, while Larry Ince had made his escape upon the late, unlamented Billy Jackson's tan gelding.

"Wa'al, I ain't gonna go fetch them saddlebags, not till I've got me some clothes on," said Ablett.

"Nor me," grinned Stone.

Both men were barefoot, the Kentuckian clad only in his denim pants and Ray

Ablett in his shirt-tails. Consequently, they hurriedly closed the kitchen door and headed for their respective bedrooms, intending to dress as quickly as possible. En route, Stone stopped outside Sally McBride's bedroom and tapped on the door.

"Who is it?" cried a nervous voice from within.

"It's me, Stone. The shootin's over an' you ain't got nuthin' more to worry 'bout. One of them buffalo hunters has took off with the bank robber. The other I shot dead. That's the good news."

"An' the bad news?" enquired Sally anxiously.

"Seems they laid the sheriff out. Dunno how bad he's hurt. Also, they shot an' killed some feller who was lurkin' in the kitchen. You wouldn't know anythin' 'bout him, I s'pose?"

Sally gasped and, in a sobbing voice, replied, "He's the . . . the feller I told you 'bout, Pete Sangster. He arrived here last night. He'd been followin' me an' them buffalo hunters since we quit Clinton Falls. We . . . we was gonna ride off together jest as soon as the blizzard ended."

"Yeah, I figured as much," said Stone. "Wa'al, you an' Grey Dove git yoreselves dressed, an' then we'll sort things out."

In the event, things were sorted out pretty quickly. Sheriff Daniel Budge, being young and pretty darned tough, soon recovered from the blow dealt him by Larry Ince. And, while Jack Stone and Ray Ablett dressed, he went out into the snow and fetched his horse. He took the saddlebags off the animal's back and gave them and their contents to the Kentuckian for safe keeping, saying he proposed to ride out after the two miscreants.

"I aim to bring them murderin' varmints to book an', at the same time, recover the rest of the money stolen from the Cattlemen's Bank at Barton's Ford," he declared.

Stone frowned. The young sheriff

had pursued Roscoe Cutter and his cousin and taken them unawares. But he was unlikely to catch Cutter off guard a second time. Cutter and the buffalo hunter would almost certainly be heading up into the Stillwater Mountains, perfect country for lying in ambush. It would be all too easy for them to bushwhack Daniel Budge.

"I cain't let you go alone," said Stone.

"Whaddya mean?" cried Budge.

"If 'n' I do, those sonsofbitches'll lie in wait for you an' pick you off easier 'n shootin' targets at a fair."

"Mr Stone's right. They'll kill you for sure," said Ray Ablett.

"I took Cutter an' his previous pardner without no trouble," retorted Budge.

"So, this time, the bastards will be expectin' you," said Stone.

The Kentuckian had no wish to involve himself in the pursuit of the two fugitives, yet he felt he had no choice other than to ride along with the young sheriff. Daniel Budge's children had lost their mother in tragic circumstances. Stone was determined that they should not lose their father.

"I think it would be best if you accepted Mr Stone's offer of help," interjected Sally McBride quietly.

Daniel Budge stared at the blonde and then nodded. What the Kentuckian had said made sense.

"Okay, I . . . I 'preciate that. It's jest that it ain't yore fight an' I don't like involvin' you in it," he murmured.

"That's all right. Guess I'm makin' it my fight," said Stone.

Thus the Kentuckian's participation in the chase was settled, and, after a short discussion, it was decided that the saddlebags should be left in Ray Ablett's care. The saloonkeeper also undertook to take the bodies of Pete Sangster and Jim Wade out to Boot Hill and bury them there.

Grey Dove was unhappy at being left behind, but Stone eventually persuaded her to remain at Silver Seam under

Sally's protection. The blonde, although still distraught at the death of her lover, readily agreed to look after the little Paiute girl, and Stone guessed that they would probably comfort each other.

Daniel Budge appropriated Jim Wade's Colt Peacemaker and, once he and the Kentuckian had mounted their horses and prepared to depart, Stone turned and addressed Sally. He had given a promise to Two Elks and he intended to keep it, whatever happened.

"Guess you'll be headin' for either Reno or Carson City?" he said.

"That's right. One or the other," said Sally.

"Then, do me a favour. I ain't aimin' to git myself shot, but, jest in case I do, I wanta be sure Grey Dove gits to her grandpa, White Cloud, who's chief of the Paiute tribe camped over at Battle Mountain."

"That's a ways north from here an', to git there, you gotta travel through some pretty wild country. I don't think

I . . . " began Sally.

"I ain't askin' you to take her," said Stone. "All I'm askin', is you head for Carson City rather than Reno. There's a feller there called Seth Burgess, who runs a general store on Main Street. We used to be Army scouts together, an' he owes me a favour. He'll take Grey Dove to Battle Mountain if 'n' you tell him it's to oblige me."

"Sure thing, Mr Stone. If the need arises. But I've got a feelin' you'll be takin' her there yoreself," replied the blonde.

"I certainly hope so, Miss Sally," said the Kentuckian, with a grin.

7

RIDING up through the Stillwater Mountains is hard work at any time of the year. But riding through the mountains that March, with a bitter wind blowing and the snow in some places well above the horses' fetlocks, was hellishly difficult. Consequently, progress was painfully slow. Roscoe Cutter and Larry Ince kept going, but they were not happy men. A quick, easy dash for Oregon was what they would have cheerfully settled for. However, that was out of the question. The only consolation was that the conditions would be just as difficult for their pursuer.

As they headed on up into the mountains, they kept forever looking back over their shoulders for any sight of Daniel Budge, for they were convinced that the young sheriff, once he recovered consciousness, would set off on their trail. Cutter reckoned Budge might possibly have settled for the retrieval of half the bank haul had not Billy Jackson gunned down his wife. Her death, though, had made it inconceivable that the sheriff should halt until he had settled matters with Cutter. He would, therefore, pursue them — relentlessly.

Roscoe Cutter turned in the saddle for the umpteenth time and stared back along the trail. The snow had long since ceased, there was a clear, blue sky overhead and visibility was excellent. Cutter looked long and hard, but there was no sign of pursuit. Not that that reassured the bank robber, for, since leaving the plain, they had traversed forests, ravines and all manner of rough country, where a smart, intelligent pursuer might easily be keeping out of sight.

"I've been thinkin'," he growled.

"Oh, yeah? What about?" asked his companion.

"'Bout that there sheriff," said Cutter.

"Mebbe he's still out for the count?" chuckled Larry Ince.

"Nope. You didn't hit him that hard," retorted Cutter. "No, I feel it in my bones that he's out there somewheres."

"He could be miles back. Hell, we keep goin', we're sure to cross the state line 'fore he catches up!"

"If we make it through these darned mountains."

"Why in tarnation shouldn't we?"

"The high passes are almost sure to be snowbound. We may find them impassable."

"Wa'al, we gotta give it a try. I ain't no gunslinger an' so don't fancy no shoot-out with the sheriff. No, we gotta make it to Oregon. Then we'll be outa his jurisdiction."

"That won't stop him."

"You reckon?"

"I know. He wants revenge for the death of his wife, an' he ain't gonna give up till he gits it."

"Wa'al, that ain't nuthin' to do with me."

"The sheriff ain't likely to see it that way, not while yo're ridin' with me."

"We could split up."

"We could, though I've a better idea." Roscoe Cutter grinned wickedly and pointed to a narrow defile not a hundred yards ahead of them. "Let's find ourselves a good hidin'-place in that there gorge an' jest sit an' wait. An' you needn't worry 'bout no shoot-out. He'll be a sittin' duck."

Larry Ince laughed harshly.

"I like it," he chortled. "He's gotta follow our trail pretty goddam closely or he could lose us. So, he's sure to pursue us into the gorge."

"Yeah. The sonofabitch will ride straight into our li'l ambush," rasped Cutter.

The two men were still laughing as they rode into the mouth of the rocky defile.

They were not to know, however, that Sheriff Daniel Budge had an ally,

163

that the famous Kentuckian gunfighter, Jack Stone, was riding with him. And Stone had a vast experience of pursuing wanted felons and bringing them to book. He always tried to put himself in his quarry's boots and figure out what he was thinking. This was a stratagem which had paid off many times in the past, and one which, in present circumstances, Stone was again attempting.

The long haul across the snow-laden plain and on up into the mountains had been made mostly in silence. Stone had been busy trying to out-think their quarry, while Budge's thoughts were concentrated upon the murder of his beloved wife and what he would do without her. He was lost in these sad, unhappy thoughts when, suddenly, Stone's voice roused him from his reverie.

"Wa'al, Sheriff, what would you do if you was them no-account critters we're pursuin'?" enquired the Kentuckian.

"Er? Er . . . whaddya mean?" Daniel

Budge hastily collected himself and mumbled, "If I was them, I'd . . . er . . . hope to make it through the Stillwater Mountains an' then ride hell-for-leather for Oregon, I guess."

"The high passes are likely to be blocked until such time as the snow begins to thaw."

"So? It's late March an' . . . "

"An' as cold as charity. That wind's gonna have to drop, an' the temperature is gonna have to rise pretty darned fast, for all that snow to melt."

"Wa'al, if they turn back, they're almost certain to ride slap-bang into us."

"Unless they stay put."

"Stay put?"

"That's what I'd do if I was them. I'd find a good spot for an ambush an' then jest settle down an' wait."

"That's what you suggested they'd do back in Silver Seam."

"Yup. An' the territory ahead of us is perfect for layin' in ambush."

Daniel Budge glanced round him. So

far, they had reached only the foothills. Ahead of them, the trail wound its way through forest and ravines, up into the mountains. And that was the way they must go if they were to continue following the tracks of the two desperadoes. So far, it had been easy. The snow had made it so. A five-year-old could have tracked Roscoe Cutter and Larry Ince without the slightest difficulty.

"Wa'al, whaddya reckon?" enquired Daniel Budge, shooting an anxious glance at the big, broadshouldered Kentuckian.

"I figure we gotta split up," commented Stone.

"So, what do we do?"

"I'm afraid yo're gonna have the dangerous job. I want you to carry on along the trail as though yo're suspectin' nuthin'. I, meanwhile, will ride up onto the high ground an' take a parallel course along the ridges. From up there, I should be able to look down on the trail an' pick out anyone waitin' in ambush. Then, it'll be up to me to shoot the sonsofbitches 'fore they can draw a bead on you."

"Yeah, wa'al, I'd like the bank robber to be taken alive, for I want that bastard to swing."

Stone smiled wryly and replied, "That may not be possible, Sheriff. We cain't pussyfoot about here. Otherwise it's you an' me who will end up dead."

Budge sighed and nodded. His face was pale and drawn, a look of grim determination etched across his youthful features. He realised that the Kentuckian was right and, while he badly wanted Cutter to hang, he was astute enough to recognise that the chances of taking the bank robber alive were slim.

"Okay," he said quietly.

Stone clapped him on the shoulder.

"Gimme twenty minutes to climb up onto the first ridge," said the Kentuckian. "Then, head on along the trail, an' we'll see if we've guessed right."

Daniel Budge pulled an ancient time-piece from his vest pocket, it had been his father's, and consulted it carefully. The waiting seemed like an eternity, but eventually the twenty minutes passed and he resumed his journey. As he rode along, he cast the occasional glance upwards to the rim of whichever ravine he happened to be passing through. But of the Kentuckian there was no sign.

The two men had been parted for the best part of two hours when Daniel Budge approached a narrow defile. It was by no means the first that he had encountered, yet, as he drew closer, he felt the hairs on the back of his neck begin to rise. Instinctively, he felt that danger lurked within its narrow confines.

Slowly, he trotted through the snow up to the mouth of the desolate, rock-strewn gorge. There were a dozen or more possible hiding-places within the first fifty yards. Budge shot anxious glances in the direction of each and every one of them, his right hand hovering an inch or two above the butt of his Colt Peacemaker.

By the time he was sixty yards down the gorge, the sheriff was starting to tell himself that his instincts had perhaps misled him. He could not, however, entirely banish the eerie feeling that he was being watched. His nervousness refused to subside. His hand continued to hover above the butt of his revolver. Digging his heels into the roan's flanks, he quickened his pace and, as he did so, a shot suddenly rang out. The bullet whistled past Daniel Budge's left ear, and he was out of the saddle and crouching down among a tumble of boulders in a matter of seconds.

Another couple of shots were promptly aimed at him, both ricocheting away off the boulder behind which he crouched. At the same time, Jack Stone opened fire from the rim of the gorge. He had been scanning it for any sign of the ambushers, but, until the outlaw and the buffalo hunter began shooting, he had been unable to spot them.

Now he sent a volley of shots into the small, rocky enclave in which they were hiding. The rifle shots bounced off the walls of their natural refuge and sent the two men scuttling out into the open, where Daniel Budge was able to blast away at them from behind his barrier of boulders. Caught between the crossfire of Daniel Budge's Colt Peackmaker and Jack Stone's Winchester, the pair had no chance.

Roscoe Cutter was hit in the shoulder by one of the sheriff's slugs and, immediately afterwards, in the back by a shell from Stone's Winchester. The former passed right through his body, breaking his collar-bone in passing, while the latter struck and shattered his spine. As he staggered and fell forward, a third shot struck him behind the left ear and blasted his brains out through his forehead. He slipped sideways onto the snow and lay quite still.

The buffalo hunter fared little better. He succeeded in grazing the sheriff's right arm with one shot, and would undoubtedly have plugged him with his next, but, before he could again squeeze the trigger, Stone sent a slug thudding into his neck. It ripped through flesh and sinew and erupted from the front of his throat, blasting out his Adam's apple. As Larry Ince fell onto his knees, coughing up great mouthfuls of blood, the sheriff pumped two more bullets into him, one of which pierced his heart and killed him instantly.

By the time the Kentuckian joined him in the gorge, Daniel Budge had rounded up the horses and checked to see that the saddlebags, containing the remainder of the bank's money, were thrown across the back of one of them.

"Whaddya reckon we should do 'bout them?" he asked, indicating the two corpses.

"Leave 'em to the buzzards," said Stone. "Ain't that what you did to that feller's pardner?"

"Yup."

"Wa'al, then, let's leave 'em an' head on back to Silver Seam."

Daniel Budge nodded.

"Okay," he said, "let's do that."

And so it was that Roscoe Cutter and Larry Ince remained lying in the gorge, to become meat for buzzards, coyotes and bears, while the sheriff and the Kentuckian headed back towards the ghost town of Silver Seam. Stone led the way, with Budge following and leading the two riderless horses.

In this manner, they rode down from the mountains and southward across the plain, travelling non-stop until eventually darkness fell. Thereupon, they made camp on the edge of a stand of cottonwood, where they lit a fire and enjoyed a supper of hot, black coffee and roasted deer, a young fawn having been spotted and shot by Stone.

At first light, they rose and breakfasted on the cold remains of the deer and drank some fresh coffee. Then they remounted and began the last stage of their journey. Neither man said much as they rode along. Jack Stone was taciturn by nature, while Daniel Budge was once more lost in his private thoughts.

8

IT was mid-morning on the day following Stone's and the sheriff's departure and the occupants of the Silver Dollar Saloon were anxiously awaiting their return. They did not know how long it would have taken the two men to catch up with their quarry, but they suspected it would not be more than a few hours. They prayed that Stone and the sheriff had survived the encounter and would shortly be riding back into Silver Seam.

Suddenly, they heard the sound of horses' hooves. These seemed to emanate from the far end of the town and to be slowly approaching the saloon. There were relieved smiles all round, and Ray Ablett quickly crossed the bar-room and stepped outside onto the stoop. It was not, however, the Kentuckian and the sheriff who were entering the ghost town. It was a troop of bluecoated US Cavalry, led by Captain George Riley.

The soldiers, having survived the blizzard of the night before last, and having had little rest and little food since, were not exactly in the pink of condition. The tall, hawk-faced captain, his sergeant and some of the tougher, more experienced troopers did not seem to have fared too badly, but the young lieutenant, the wounded and a number of the younger, less hard-bitten troopers looked close to the point of exhaustion. Cold and hungry, they were both amazed and delighted to see Ray Ablett step out through the saloon's batwing doors.

Captain George Riley raised his hand and brought the troop to a halt in front of the saloon.

"This is a pleasant surprise, mister!" he exclaimed. "For I figured this here town to be deserted."

"Wa'al, I'm its last resident. An' I'm reckonin' on moseyin' on out come this spring," said Ablett.

"That cain't be far off."

"Nope. As soon as these snows melt, I'll be on my way."

"In the meantime, can you provide me an' my men with a li'l sustenance?" enquired Riley.

"I guess so," said Ablett.

"Splendid!" cried the captain, and, turning in the saddle, he yelled, "Troop, dismount!"

The soldiers took no second bidding. The Silver Dollar Saloon seemed to them a veritable Paradise after their terrible journey. Even those troopers, who were wounded and almost totally exhausted, succeeded in tumbling off their horses and staggering up the steps onto the stoop. Then, they trooped into the saloon behind their captain. A gaunt, palefaced Lieutenant Ben Nicholson brought up the rear in company with Sergeant Frank Collins. The sergeant kept a fatherly eye on the young subaltern, for he had been impressed by the youngster's fortitude and considered that, with experience, Nicholson could make a good and able officer.

Inside the saloon, Sally McBride had brought some knives and forks through from the kitchen, in anticipation of the return of Jack Stone and the young sheriff. She paused in the act of laying them down on one of the tables, surprised and disappointed to see Riley and his troopers entering the bar-room instead of the two men she had expected.

Grey Dove had been on the point of following her into the bar-room, but, upon seeing George Riley, she quickly shut the door and retreated, as fast as her little legs would carry her, along the corridor and back to the kitchen. Sally was not slow to notice this. Was it, she wondered, simply a fear of anyone in an Army bluecoat that had precipitated Grey Dove's hasty retreat, or was it, perhaps, fear of the actual bluecoats who had massacred her family and friends?

"Now, then, Mr . . . er . . . ?" began Riley.

"Ablett. Ray Ablett, proprietor of this here saloon," said the saloonkeeper.

"Wa'al, Mr Ablett, my name's George Riley, Cap'n George Riley. An' me an' my men have been out combin' the territory, lookin' for a bunch of renegade Injuns who've been terrorisin' an' murderin' honest, God-fearin' white folks." Riley paused and then continued with a grin, "You'll be glad to hear we caught the red bastards, an' that they won't be troublin' nobody in future."

"Which renegade band was this?" enquired Sally.

"Wolf's Tail an' his Shoshones," replied Riley.

"Yeah. An' we also gave them Paiutes one helluva lesson!" laughed Joe Shaughnessy.

Riley glowered at the corporal. He had no wish that anyone outside the Army should know of the massacre in Duck Valley. Indeed, upon his return to Fort McDermitt, he would have to be very careful in the wording of his report if he were to avoid a reprimand.

"I didn't realise the Paiutes were givin' us any trouble," said Sally innocently.

"Another renegade band," retorted Riley shortly.

"Oh, an' jest where did you catch up with them?" enquired the blonde.

"In Duck Valley," said Ben Nicholson in a low voice.

"I see you took no prisoners," observed Sally.

"No," said Nicholson, staring down at the floor and, thus, avoiding the girl's eye.

"Anyways, you said you could provide my troops an' me with some food, Mr Ablett," remarked Riley, adroitly changing the subject, "So, if you an' yore wife . . . "

Ray Ablett laughed.

"Hell, Miss Sally ain't my wife!" he declared.

"No?"

"No, sir. Like I said, I'm the last resident of this here ghost town. I stayed put when the silver ran out last December, Miss Sally, she arrived here a couple days back an' is simply passin' through, jest like you an' yore men.

"Is that a fact?"

"It is," confirmed Sally.

"An' how did you come to arrive in this Godforsaken spot, all on yore lonesome?" demanded Riley curiously.

"It's a long story."

"Wa'al, I ain't in no special hurry."

"Very well, Cap'n," said Sally. "It was like this." And she went on to describe the events of the last few days, including the infamous poker game in which she had been won by the buffalo hunter, Jim Wade. The one thing she did not mention, however, was the fact that Jack Stone had been accompanied by Grey Dove, whom he was proposing to take to the Paiute reservation at Battle Mountain. Instead, she merely said that the Kentuckian had indicated he was on his way to Carson City.

She was afraid that Ray Ablett might intervene and apprise the cavalry captain of the Indian girl's presence. However, he did not and eventually she concluded her tale by saying, "So, y'see, Cap'n, me an' Mr Ablett are anxiously awaitin' the return of Mr Stone an' Sheriff Budge."

"Yeah. Wa'al, let's hope they make out okay against them two thievin' varmints," said Riley. "But, meantime, hows 'bout rustlin' up that there food we spoke of?"

"Sure thing. Will pork 'n' beans suit you?" enquired Ray Ablett.

"That'll suit us jest dandy. An' we'll be wantin' somethin' to drink."

"We got plenty of pipin' hot coffee."

"I was thinkin' of somethin' a mite stronger, like whiskey."

"Wa'al, I was figurin' on providin' the food an' the coffee free of charge," said Ablett. "But, as for the whiskey, I'm gonna need that to help secure my future when I leave here an' make for Carson City. It'll fetch quite a few dollars there an . . . "

"That's okay. We'll be happy to pay for the whiskey," said Riley.

"In cash?" asked Ablett.

"Hell, no! Like I told you, we're on duty, Injun fightin'. We ain't carryin' no cash. But jest bring me a pen an' ink an' a sheet of paper, an' I'll sign a requisition, which you can present to the Army for payment."

"An' where exactly are you an' yore men stationed, Cap'n?"

"At Fort McDermitt."

"Hmm. That's a good ways north of here. I wasn't figurin' on makin' no journey up yonder."

"You won't need to. You can present yore bill at the Army establishment nearest to Carson City."

Ray Ablett nodded. He was not at all happy with this arrangement, for he realised it could be a very long-winded process. Indeed, it would probably be months before he got his money, if he ever got it. Nonetheless, he was afraid to defy the captain. He recognised that Captain George Riley would be a bad man to cross and, so, reluctantly, he agreed to let Riley requisition the whiskey.

"Okay," he said. "I'll . . . er . . . bring some paper an' a pen an' ink, an' . . . "

"There's no hurry. We can deal with the paperwork later. For the moment, hadn't you an' Miss Sally better head for the kitchen an' fix us that meal?" said Riley.

"But . . . but I'll need to tend the bar!"

"No, that's okay. Corporal Shaughnessy can act as bartender."

"But . . . "

"You do trust us to keep count? You ain't afraid we'll cheat you, are yuh?"

Ray Ablett swallowed hard. That was exactly what he feared, yet he dared not say so.

"Er . . . no . . . no. I'm . . . er . . . sure I can trust you to let me know how much of my whiskey stock you an' yore men consume, Cap'n," he stammered.

"'Course you can," said Riley, his voice soft, but his eyes showing only too clearly the contempt he felt for his host.

"C'mon, Miss Sally, let's go fix that meal," muttered Ablett, and he and the blonde hurried from the bar-room.

As they left, Joe Shaughnessy slipped behind the bar-counter and reached for a whiskey bottle, and Riley and some of the rougher elements burst into raucous laughter at the saloonkeeper's obvious discomfiture.

Lieutenant Ben Nicholson and Sergeant Frank Collins, meanwhile, began to tend to the wounded. The four seriously wounded were in a very poor way, for they had suffered badly in the blizzard and had little or no rest since. The other five wounded could have been better, but were certainly no worse than one or two of their comrades whom the dreadful conditions of the last few days had also adversely affected. Lieutenant Nicholson prayed that the weather would quickly improve. Otherwise, he was afraid that a number of the troopers would not survive the journey back to Fort McDermitt.

Ray Ablett and Sally McBride both heaved a sigh of relief as Sally closed the door behind them and they made their way along the narrow passage to the kitchen. There they found Grey Dove crouching beside the table, her father's lance held at the ready. Her face was wet with tears and her dark eyes wide with fear.

"I reckon she recognised Cap'n George Riley as the officer whose men raided her village an' massacred her folks," said Sally.

"Sure she did," agreed Ablett grimly.

Sally smiled sadly at the little Paiute.

"You don't need to be afraid, honey," she said quietly. "We don't let those sonsofbitches hurt you."

The blonde's reassuring smile and soft words had a comforting effect upon the Indian girl, although she did not understand their exact meaning, Grey

Dove replied with a shy smile. She did not, however, relinquish her grasp of the lance.

"I jest hope we can protect her from those soldiers," muttered Ablett, pulling nervously on his long, drooping moustache.

"So long as none of 'em comes into the kitchen, they ain't to know she's here," said Sally.

"I s'pose not."

"An' there ain't no reason why any of 'em should poke their heads in here."

"You reckon?"

"I reckon, partickerly as they'll be kinda busy guzzlin' yore liquor."

"Thanks for remindin' me," growled Ablett, and this time it was his turn to smile, albeit wryly.

"Don't mention it," said Sally, as she lifted down a saucepan from its shelf.

While Sally and the saloonkeeper were busily engaged in cooking their meal, Captain George Riley and his troop of US Cavalrymen were happily swigging Ray Ablett's whiskey. With the exception of Lieutenant Nicholson, Sergeant Collins, some of the wounded, and a few of the younger troopers, they knocked back the red-eye as though it were water. Joe Shaughnessy, as bartender, made sure he had his share, while their commander drank more than anyone.

Luckily, George Riley had a strong head for liquor, since the amount he consumed would easily have floored a lesser man. Nevertheless, he was far from sober when, eventually, Ablett and the blonde reappeared, bearing the food and coffee. They placed a copious helping of pork and beans in front of each soldier, and then they went round and poured each of them a mug of strong, black coffee.

The soldiers set to with gusto and soon demolished the food that had been placed before them. The offer of second helpings was accepted by a few, while everyone thankfully accepted another mug of coffee. Then, as Sally and the saloonkeeper turned to leave the bar-room and return to the sanctuary of the kitchen, Joe Shaughnessy staggered drunkenly to his feet and planted himself between them and the door. He leered at the blonde, his craggy, bearded face split into a broad, lustful grin.

"Will you please excuse us?" said Sally, trying hard not to show her distaste.

"No, I don't reckon I will," replied the big, bear-like corporal.

"Wh . . . whaddya mean?" demanded Ablett nervously.

"I mean, you can go, but the woman stays here."

"Cap'n, this . . . this is an outrage!" cried Ablett, as he eyed Corporal Shaughnessy with some trepidation.

George Riley smiled and put down his coffee cup. He slowly rose and faced the soldier.

"What's the idea, Corporal?" he asked.

"Wa'al, sir, I've had me some whiskey, an' I've had me, some chuck.

An' now I fancy havin' a woman."

"This woman?"

"That's right. After all, she ain't nuthin' but a goddam whore."

"Is that true?"

Riley's question was directed at Sally, but, before she could reply, Shaughnessy rasped, "'Course it's true, sir. Trooper Devlin has seen her workin' the Pleasure Palace in Reno. Ain't that right, Charley?"

"It sure is. I recognised her straight away," declared Charley Devlin, a small, sandy-haired man who, before joining the army, had pursued the same profession as the late lamented Pete Sangster.

"Wa'al, whaddya say to that, Miss Sally?" said Riley.

"I . . . I have earned my livin' as a saloon girl, yes, but . . . " began the blonde.

"As a whore. Let's use the correct term," Riley interrupted her.

"Look, where's this leadin'? Miss Sally ain't workin' for me. She's jest

189

passin' through," said Ray Ablett.

"Shuddup!" snapped Riley.

"But . . . "

"I'm warnin' you. Jest shuddup!" yelled Riley.

Ablett blanched. He feared that the cavalry captain was an ugly customer at the best of times. Filled with whiskey, George Riley was about as unpredictable and dangerous as a rampaging grizzly.

"Yessir," muttered the saloonkeeper timorously.

Riley grinned and turned his attention to Sally, who stood looking longingly, past the immense bulk of Joe Shaughnessy, at the door through which she wanted so much to pass.

"Wa'al, seein' as how yo're a sportin' woman," he said, carefully using that term instead of the rather more pejorative word, 'whore', "I reckon you cain't rightly refuse yore services to this fine, upstandin' soldier."

While he spoke, the fine, upstanding soldier, who was noticeably swaying, belched loudly and staggered back a few paces.

"I . . . I think, sir, that this has gone far enough," said Ben Nicholson, stepping up to his superior officer and addressing him in a quiet, confidential voice.

"Do you indeed?" Riley turned and fixed the subaltern with a murderous glare. "Wa'al, let me tell you, Lieutenant, I'm in command here, an' I'll decide when things have gone far enough," he rasped.

"But, Cap'n . . . "

"Not another word, Lieutenant. That's an order."

The two men stared angrily at each other, Nicholson wanting to continue his protest, yet, in the face of the other's direct order, not daring to do so. Riley smiled suddenly, a cruel, malicious smile, and then he turned again to the blonde.

"Please, Cap'n," she whispered. "I cain't."

"Oh, but you can!" said Riley.

"'Deed, I would say it was yore patriotic duty to give yore services to any of these men who may require them. After all, haven't they been layin' their lives on the line, defendin' you an' yore fellow-citizens from the ravages of the red man?"

This remark brought forth a roar of approval from the troopers. Half-drunk and naturally excited by the blonde's rare beauty, they were all at once filled with an uncontrollable lust for her.

"Gee, can I have her, sir?"

"An' me!"

"An' me!"

One after another, the troopers yelled out, until, finally, their commander raised his hand to silence them.

"'Course you can have her, men," said Riley, with a grin, adding, "Guess we'll have to draw lots to see who gits her first."

"No!"

Sally's agonised cry, and the look of sheer horror on her pale face, caused Ray Ablett to make an ill-advised attempt to rescue her. He made a dash for the bar, behind which he kept his scattergun. However, Riley was too quick for him. The captain might have been a little the worse for drink, yet he was by no means hopelessly drunk, and he was swift to guess what the saloonkeeper had in mind. Consequently, before Ablett could lay a hand upon the scattergun, Riley had drawn his Army Model Colt and jabbed it into the saloonkeeper's ribs.

"Jest try pickin' up that gun, an' I'll blast a hole in you big 'nough to stick my fist in," snarled Riley.

Ablett slowly withdrew his hand from its position a few inches off the barrel of the shotgun. He straightened up and, with Riley's revolver still prodding him in the ribs, stepped back into the bar-room. Then he turned and the two men stood facing each other.

"This . . . this ain't right," gasped Ablett, his face drained of all colour.

"You lecturin' me, mister?" hissed Riley.

"Er . . . no. I'm jest sayin' that mebbe you . . . aaagh!"

Ray Ablett's words ended in an anguished scream, as the captain suddenly lashed out and struck him across the face with the barrel of his Colt revolver. Ablett staggered backwards and followed up with another blow, this time splitting open the saloonkeeper's other cheek. A third blow broke his nose and, howling in agony, Ablett fell to his knees. A fourth blow aimed at his unprotected skull was deflected by Sergeant Frank Collins, who hastily stepped forward and grasped the captain by the arm.

"What in tarnation d'you think yo're doin', Sergeant?" yelled Riley.

"Stoppin' you killin' the feller, Cap'n," replied Collins tersely.

"Yes. He's had enough, sir. Look at him," added an ashenfaced Ben Nicholson.

Riley peered down at the bloodied mask that was Ray Ablett's face. Blood poured from gashes in both cheeks and from his broken nose. The saloonkeeper bent forward, leaning on his hands and moaning softly.

"Okay," Riley rasped and, carefully wiping the blood off the barrel of his revolver, he replaced it in its holster.

"Wa'al, are we gonna have that draw, Cap'n?" enquired Joe Shaughnessy gleefully.

"Sure we are," said Riley. He glanced at Sally and murmured, "Reckon we'll see what kinda sportin' woman you really are!"

Sally gazed back at him with imploring, frightened eyes. She had been with many men, both before and during her relationship with Pete Sangster, earning a living either for herself or for the two of them. But that had been her choice and she had decided where and when she worked. This time, she had no choice in the matter, and the prospect of servicing an entire troop of horny, sex-starved troopers, one after the other, filled her with unmitigated horror. She might, as

Shaughnessy had so elegantly put it, be 'a goddam whore', yet what Riley planned was nothing short of rape.

"Surely, as an officer an' a gen'lman, you cain't be serious 'bout this?" she cried.

"Oh, but I am serious!" replied Riley, whereupon he turned to his sergeant and snapped, "Right, Sergeant Collins, you'd best organise this here draw, for the men are gittin' mighty restless, an' I don't blame 'em."

"No!" screamed Sally. "No, you cain't do this to me!"

9

THE wind seemed a little less keen, and the sun shone out of a bright, blue sky as the two riders approached the one-time mining town. It was late morning, and Jack Stone and the young sheriff had made good time despite the snow, which, in some places along the trail, was extremely deep.

"Seems Silver Seam has had some visitors since we've been gone," growled Stone, pointing at the myriad hoof-marks in the snow.

"Gee, that's one helluva lot of horses!" commented Daniel Budge.

"Yup."

The Kentuckian guessed at once that the marks had been made by a troop of US Cavalry. Either that or a very large posse. As he and Budge trotted round from behind the high bluff at the northern end of town, he saw and immediately recognised the horses as belonging to the Army. He had, in his time, spent some months as an Army scout and had fought in the Civil War, and he knew an Army horse when he saw one. What in tarnation, Stone asked himself, was a troop of US Cavalry doing riding into a ghost town in the middle of nowhere? He was suddenly filled with apprehension, for he had a premonition that it was the same troop that had ridden into Duck Valley and massacred Grey Dove's family and everyone else in the Paiute village.

"Somethin' troublin' you, Mr Stone?" enquired the young sheriff, upon observing his companion's grim expression.

"Yeah, there is," replied Stone. "I gotta feelin' that those hosses belong to the troopers who raided Grey Dove's village."

"No! Hell, there ain't no reason to think that!"

"Two troops of US Cavalry in the

same territory within a few days of each other. You think that's likely, do yuh, Sheriff?"

"No, Mr Stone, guess not. But, even so . . . "

Daniel Budge's words were cut short by the sound of an anguished cry, the cry of a man in pain, coming from inside the Silver Dollar Saloon. The two men urged their horses forward and galloped up to within a few yards of the saloon. Then, they swiftly dismounted and tethered the gelding and the roan next to the troopers' horses. Drawing their guns, they hurried up onto the stoop and peered in over the batwing doors.

What they saw and heard filled them with, firstly, horror and repugnance, and, secondly, a burning anger. They observed the saloonkeeper kneeling on the floor, his face smothered in blood. And they listened as Captain George Riley threatened Sally. Although they had not heard what had gone before, they heard enough to guess at his intentions. As Sally made her final protest, they looked at each other and simultaneously cocked their revolvers.

In response to Sally's protest, Riley merely laughed and retorted harshly, "I can, an' will, do jest what I like with you. An' so, you may be sure, will my men."

"I don't think so," rasped Stone, and he and the sheriff stepped smartly through the batwing doors and into the bar-room.

George Riley's mouth fell open, as he observed the tall, tough-looking Kentuckian and the grim-faced young sheriff standing there in the doorway. Both Jack Stone's Frontier Model Colt and Daniel Budge's Colt Peacemaker were aimed directly at his heart.

"Who in tarnation are you?" demanded Riley, although he guessed they were the two men of whom Sally and Ablett had spoken earlier.

"My name's Jack Stone an' this here's Sheriff Daniel Budge," rasped the Kentuckian.

"Yeah. An' we'd like to know what's goin' on here?" said Budge.

"They . . . they're plannin' to rape Miss Sally," cried Ray Ablett, attempting unsuccessfully to rise to his feet.

Riley shot a venomous look at the saloonkeeper and made as though to aim a kick at him.

"I wouldn't if 'n' I was you," snapped Stone.

Riley slowly lowered his foot and turned to face the Kentuckian.

"Look, mister, this is Army business, an' you an' the sheriff would do well to keep yore goddam noses outa it!" he hissed.

"No! Please, please help me!" sobbed Sally.

"Don't worry, ma'am. None of these sonsofbitches is gonna so much as touch you," growled Stone.

Riley laughed shortly and said, "Be sensible, fellers, you cain't hope to out-shoot this entire troop. You'll die for certain."

"But not before we take out a whole

heap of yore men," said Stone. "An', believe me, yo're gonna be the first to go."

"That's right, Cap'n. Nuthin' would give me greater pleasure than to pump a slug into yore stinkin' heart," added Daniel Budge.

"Is that so?" Riley calculated that the range was too long for either the Kentuckian or the sheriff to hit him with their six-guns. From where they stood, just inside the doorway of the saloon, they would certainly be capable of gunning down quite a few of the troopers, but he figured that he would not be among those shot. "I daresay yo're a couple hot-shots, but you ain't gonna hit me from that distance," he stated firmly.

"No, but I am from here!"

Riley hastily swung round and found himself staring into the barrel of Ray Ablett's shotgun. While he and his men's attention had been directed at the two gunfighters, the saloonkeeper had succeeded in crawling behind the bar and grabbing hold of the gun. Then, with a supreme effort, Ablett had staggered to his feet and, leaning upon the bar-counter for support, was now aiming the scattergun straight at the cavalry captain.

"Don't be a fool, mister," snapped Riley. "You wanta die, you jest try squeezin' that trigger."

"Don't tempt me," snarled Ablett.

Frank Collins stared at the saloon-keeper's battered, bloodied face and saw murder writ large in Ablett's eyes.

"He means it, Cap'n. For God's sake, let the girl go. She ain't worth the trouble," he growled.

Riley scowled.

"I ain't gonna be dictated to by a bunch of civilians," he stated.

"But, sir, s'pose you do survive, what in tarnation are you gonna tell Colonel Cameron? That you lost 'bout a third of yore men in a bar-room shoot-out over some whore?"

"The sergeant is right, Cap'n," interjected Ben Nicholson. "You go through with this and you are finished. Either you'll be dead, or, if you survive and get back to Fort McDermitt, you'll find yourself facing a court-martial."

Riley glowered at the young subaltern. The implication in Nicholson's words was only to clear. He would in no way support his superior should Riley attempt a cover-up. Riley glanced from Nicholson to Collins. The veteran sergeant's look of cold contempt told him that he could expect no support from that quarter. Should either man be questioned about the casualties incurred during the troop's foray against Wolf's Tail and his Shoshones, they would be certain to tell Colonel Cameron exactly who had died or been wounded in the action against the Indians. And that would leave any further casualties unaccounted for. Riley cursed beneath his breath. Much against the grain, he would have to back down.

"Very well," he said grudgingly. "I s'pose the goddam whore ain't really worth fightin' over."

"Gee, Cap'n, what are yuh sayin'? I was lookin' forward to havin' me some real good sport with her!" cried Corporal Joe Shaughnessy.

"So was I!" declared a big, smiling-faced negro trooper.

"Me, too!" said Trooper Devlin.

"An' me!" yelled a third trooper.

"Yeah. Wa'al, I'm afraid you boys'll have to wait till you git back to Fort McDermitt 'fore you do any whorin'." Riley glanced from the saloonkeeper to the two men standing facing him across the length of the bar-room. "These fellers mean what they say," he muttered.

"We could shoot it out with 'em," growled Shaughnessy.

"No, I don't think so."

"But, Cap'n . . . "

"That's an order, Corporal," rasped Riley.

"Yessir."

Riley smiled thinly and turned and faced the troopers.

"You men have eaten yore fill an'

rested some, so I reckon it's time we moved on out," he stated.

He was aware that a number of the troopers, particularly the wounded, would have benefited from a much longer period of rest and recuperation. However, he also knew that he had to get the others out of Silver Seam and away from what was potentially an explosive situation. If he did not, there would almost certainly be carnage.

Lieutenant Ben Nicholson concurred with this view and wasted no time in barking out an order.

"Okay, men, get to your feet and file out of here. Then mount up. We have a long way to go," he snapped.

There were dark murmurings and angry scowls from some to the troopers, but none dared disobey the subaltern's direct order. Accordingly, they threw back the remains of their drinks. Then they rose up from their seats and began to shuffle reluctantly out of the saloon.

Stone and the sheriff stepped aside

to let them pass, but neither man lowered his gun. As for Ray Ablett, he followed a few paces behind Captain George Riley, his shotgun aimed at the bluecoated officer's back. He was still a little shaky from the beating he had taken, but he was determined not to drop his guard.

The soldiers trooped slowly, silently, out onto the stoop. The majority were thankful that a further conflict had been avoided. Only a few would willingly have tackled the Kentuckian and his two companions. Included in their number were the bloodthirsty Corporal Joe Shaughnessy, the smiling-faced negro trooper, Charley Devlin and, of course, their ruthless commanding officer, Captain George Riley.

The three civilians watched vigilantly while the troopers mounted. This took quite a few minutes, since some of the wounded had to be helped onto their horses. Presently, however, all were saddled and ready to ride. They lined up in a column of twos and, with

Captain George Riley at their head, cantered off along Main Street. Once they were beyond the town limits, they turned northwards and disappeared out of sight behind the high bluffs at the far end of the valley. Stone and the others watched them go with a profound sense of relief. But it was not until the last soldier had vanished from sight that they finally lowered their weapons.

"Good riddance!" exclaimed Ablett.

"Yessiree!" Stone grinned at the saloonkeeper and said, "Wa'al, let's go inside an' git you cleaned up."

"Yeah. You sure look as if you took one helluva beatin'," commented Daniel Budge.

"It looks worse 'nit is," replied Ablett bravely.

"Who did this to you?" enquired Stone.

"That doggone captain, the bastard!"

"I might've guessed! But don't go judgin' all Army men by him. You git a rotten apple in every barrel," said the Kentuckian.

"He was certainly a rotten apple," said Sally, who had come out onto the stoop to join the three men. "He an' his men were the murderin' sonsofbitches who massacred Grey Dove's people in Duck Valley."

"I'll be darned!" exclaimed Stone, and, with a worried frown, he asked the blonde, "Grey Dove, is she okay?"

"Yup, she's okay. She's pretty damn scared, but she's safe in the kitchen," said Sally.

"Thank the Lord for that!" sighed Stone, and he followed the others, back through the batwing doors, and into the saloon.

★ ★ ★

Captain George Riley was fuming with rage at having been outfaced by a bunch of civilians. He felt the humiliation keenly and, as he led his troop northwards in the direction of Fort McDermitt, he quietly brooded upon the matter.

He was not one to easily admit defeat, for he was both obstinate and vindictive, a man little liked by his fellow officers. He felt that his lack of education, and the fact that he had come up through the ranks, had held him back, had prevented him from attaining the rank of Major. In fact, this was not the case. It was the defects in his character that had held him back. He might be a bold, courageous Indian fighter, yet he lacked the self-discipline, the sense of responsibility and the balanced mind needed to hold high command. Indeed, his commanding officer, Colonel John Cameron, had often been heard to declare, "Give George more'n a troop to command, and he'd start a full-scale Indian war in less time that it takes to skin a rattlesnake!"

Given Riley's cruel, vindictive nature and his loathing of the red man, this was probably true. In the present circumstances, he had no intention of leaving matters as they stood. As he rode along, a plan slowly formed in his mind. A thin smile flicked across his lean, hawkish visage and, when they were no more than three miles from Silver Seam, he suddenly brought the troop to a halt.

Both Lieutenant Nicholson and Sergeant Collins rode up alongside him, anxious to learn the reason for this unexpected stop.

"Something wrong, sir?" enquired the subaltern.

"No, nuthin' is wrong, Lieutenant," replied Riley. "I simply wanted to inform you that I have decided to reconnoitre the plains to the west of here, out towards Lovelock. I want to be sure everythin' is okay in that part of the territory, that the ranchers an' homesteaders out there are havin' no trouble from the Shoshones."

"But, Cap'n, it was only the one renegade band of Shoshone Indians which was causing trouble, the band led by Wolf's Tail. And we've eliminated them," said Nicholson.

"While we're out here, it won't do no harm to check," said Riley.

"No, sir, I can appreciate that. But it will take us many miles out of our way, and I am not sure the men are in any condition to endure such a ride. Indeed, I feel it would be best if we were to head direct for Fort McDermitt."

"The lieutenant's right, Cap'n," interjected Frank Collins. "Some of the men are in a pretty bad way. Gittin' caught in that blizzard . . . "

"I take yore point, Sergeant," Riley interrupted him. "I realise that some, partickerly the wounded, are gonna struggle jest to make it back to the fort."

"Yes. What they need is a decent period of rest and recuperation, something they could have had at Silver Seam, had it not been for your outrageous behaviour there," thought Nicholson. Aloud, he said, "So, sir, if you agree that some of the men aren't up to . . . "

"I don't intend takin' the entire troop," stated Riley.

"You don't?" said Nicholson.

"Nope. Jest a few hand-picked men. That's all I'll need for my reconnaissance."

"I see."

"The rest of the troop I shall place under yore command. I am sure you an' the sergeant, between you, will see that they all git safely back to Fort McDermitt."

Ben Nicholson looked both relieved and surprised. The captain's tone was conciliatory, friendly even. After the debacle at Silver Seam, Nicholson had expected him to be more irascible than ever. He was delighted, therefore, to find Riley in such a reasonable frame of mind.

"You can rely on me, sir," he said cheerfully.

"An' on me, Cap'n," added Collins, also looking relieved.

"Good! That's settled then," said Riley. He turned to face the troopers and barked out a list of names, those whom he intended should form the patrol he proposed to lead: "Shaughnessy, Rickard, Bass, Fallon, Stark an' Devlin, you will ride with me!" he cried.

Nicholson ran an appraising eye over the six men. They were the roughest, toughest men in the troop. Shaughnessy, Rickard and Fallon were all big, bear-like ruffians, always eager for a fight. Bass was a one-time negro slave who might have been expected to sympathise with the redskins, but didn't. As for the other two, Stark and Devlin, they were both quick-tempered, foul-mouthed lunkheads, forever in trouble. Back at Fort McDermitt, all six were constantly breaking Army regulations and being punished for their misdemeanours. However, as fighting men, they were the match of any in the regiment.

Nicholson conceded that they had fought with great courage and ferocity in the battle against Wolf's Tail and his Shoshones, though he had been sickened by their savagery during the course of the massacre of the Paiutes in Duck Valley. He was not particularly unhappy, therefore, to lose them for the remainder of the journey back to the fort. After all, he had no reason to suppose the troop would encounter any trouble on the ride north.

"We'll likely catch up with you an' the rest of the troop someways along the trail," said Riley.

"And if you don't, sir?" said Nicholson.

"Wa'al, you can explain to Colonel Cameron that I thought I oughta make certain all is quiet in the western quarter of the territory, an' that I'll be along directly," said Riley. He smiled and then added, "Take it easy on the ride back to Fort McDermitt, Lieutenant, for I don't wanta lose no more men. Have a trouble-free journey, an' good luck!"

"Yessir," said Nicholson, continuing to be surprised at the captain's sudden and unexpected amiability.

The troop split into two separate columns, the larger contingent following the subaltern northwards across the plains, while Captain George Riley and his six chosen men headed off westwards, in the direction of distant Lovelock. The half-dozen troopers were not too happy at being diverted from the main trail back to Fort McDermitt. The pleasures on offer at the fort were extremely limited, but nevertheless they appealed strongly to the roughnecks riding at Riley's back. Gut-rot liquor and loose women had ever been the soldier's solace.

The seven had ridden but a mile when, upon breasting a low hill and cantering down its far side, they found themselves out of sight of Lieutenant Nicholson and the rest of the troop. As the trail levelled out at the foot of the hill, Riley once again brought his men to a halt.

"Okay, men!" he cried. "I figure none of you is exactly delighted to be participatin' in this here expedition?"

The troopers looked at one another and, finally, Joe Shaughnessy spoke up.

"Wa'al, Cap'n," he growled, "guess we'd all rather head on back to the fort."

"An' what d'you aim on doin' when you git back to the fort?" enquired Riley.

"Have me a good drink an' a nice, accommodatin' woman!" declared Shaughnessy.

"You could have both at Silver Seam. An' the woman there is a darned sight better-lookin' than any you'd lay hold of at Fort McDermitt," said Riley.

"Yo're goddam right she is!" exclaimed the negro, Bass.

The other troopers yelled their agreement. All of them had viewed Sally McBride with hot, lustful eyes, and all considered that she was an outstanding beauty, her voluptuous charms far outmatching any that the fort's batch of rough and ready whores could offer.

"Wa'al, it's my intention that we should return to Silver Seam," said Riley. "I ain't about to let them civilians git away with defyin' the US Cavalry. Hell, no! Last time, they caught us on the hop an' outmanoeuvred us. This time, we're gonna take 'em by surprise an' make 'em pay for their insolence."

Riley smiled grimly while the troopers digested this piece of information.

"So, there ain't gonna be no reconnaissance?" said Devlin.

"Nope."

"That was jest a story concocted for the benefit of Lieutenant Nicholson, wasn't it, Cap'n?" said Fallon.

"That's right."

"So, whaddya propose doin', Cap'n?" enquired Stark eagerly.

"I propose we hit that there ghost town 'fore them civilians know what's happenin'. Then, we shoot 'em up, all except the blonde. Her we're gonna need, if we're gonna have us a li'l sport. Okay, boys?"

"I cain't hardly wait, Cap'n!" roared Shaughnessy.

"Me neither!" cried Devlin.

"Nor me!" yelled Bass.

"I dunno 'bout you," said Rickard, eyeing the negro askance. "Even if she is a goddam whore, she's still a white woman, an' I don't hold with niggers screwin' white women."

Riley glared at the huge, bear-like trooper. He had forgotten that Rickard came from Texas and, indeed, was the only Southerner in the entire regiment.

"An' I don't give a damn what you hold with, Rickard," he snapped. "Yo're in the Union Army now, not the Confederate."

"You tell him, Cap'n!" cried Devlin.

Riley silenced Devlin with a cold stare. He did not need any trooper to tell him what he should do.

"Trooper Bass gits his turn jest like the rest of us," he said quietly, yet firmly.

Rickard bit his lip. He did not like it, yet he dared not defy the officer.

"You said, 'us', Cap'n. Does that mean you . . . ?" began Shaughnessy with a leer.

"Yes, Corporal. I figure that, as the only officer present, it's my bounden duty to take the first turn," grinned Riley.

This remark brought forth a roar of raucous laughter from the six troopers.

Riley waited until the laughter had died down and then stated, "As for you men, you can have her as many times as you like."

Yells of approval greeted this statement, and again Riley had to wait for the excitement to subside before adding quietly, "One small proviso, though. Since we're gonna take 'em by surprise, I ain't anticipatin' us sufferin' no casualties. However, if anyone does by chance git hisself shot, the story is, he was hit by a hostile Injun. Okay?"

The six troopers eagerly agreed. They were only too willing to go along with whatever the captain suggested. It was not just their lust for the blonde that motivated them. They, too, had felt the humiliation of being out-faced by the big Kentuckian and the young sheriff. Like Captain George Riley, they were anxious to restore their pride by returning to the ghost town and settling accounts.

Riley smiled triumphantly. He had chosen his men well. They would extract a terrible revenge, and then they would quickly catch up with the rest of the troop. And nobody, certainly not that sanctimonious prig, Lieutenant Ben Nicholson, would be any the wiser. He turned his horse's head and promptly led his men off, back in the direction of Silver Seam.

10

RAY ABLETT looked distinctly the worse for wear. Sally McBride had patched up his face as best she could, but it would be some time before the bruising and the wounds healed. And, unless he had it broken again and reset, his nose would remain forever squint. A good slug of whiskey had put the colour back into his face and he had pretty well recovered from the beating he had taken. But he no longer had any wish to linger on in Silver Seam. His original plan had been to wait until winter was over, and the snows had gone, before attempting the journey to Carson City. However, there was little likelihood of further snowfalls and, as March progressed into April, the snow which had fallen would surely begin to melt. Therefore, he determined to set forth without delay.

Ablett explained his change of mind to the others and enlisted Stone's and Budge's help to load his wagon with the remaining stores, including that whiskey which the soldiers had, thanks to the intervention of the Kentuckian and the sheriff, left unconsumed. As for the livestock, he packed the chickens in coops aboard the wagon. The cow, the pig and the buffalo hunters' mules he proposed to tether to the rear of the wagon and walk the couple of hundred or so miles to Carson City. There he intended to sell everything except his piano and, with the proceeds, buy a share in one of the city's less successful saloons, one which he could build up from scratch into a thriving business. As he recalled, few provided their customers with any kind of music, and, consequently, he figured that the piano could well prove to be integral to his success.

These plans had been long laid, as had Jack Stone's to take Grey Dove to her grandfather's reservation at Battle Mountain, and Sheriff Daniel Budge's to return the money stolen by Roscoe Cutter and Billy Jackson to the Cattlemen's Bank at Barton's Ford. Sally McBride, on the other hand, had made no real plans for her future. However, now that she was freed from her contract with the two buffalo hunters, she swiftly came to a decision. A pretty girl like her could always earn a living in a place like Carson City. She would, therefore, ask Ray Ablett if she might ride along with him. Sally smiled inwardly. The saloonkeeper was unlikely to reject such a request and, providing she played her cards right, there might be no need for her to resume her old profession. She had been impressed by, and grateful for, Ablett's attempt to intervene on her behalf, and she considered him to be an amiable and not unattractive man, whom she could easily learn to love. She had grown tired of slick, handsome ne'er-do-wells like Pete Sangster. After what she had just been through, Sally was ready for a relationship with someone who would offer her some kindness and a little stability and security.

Her mind made up, she wasted no time in putting her proposition to the saloonkeeper. As he reached down and took hold of a pile of blankets, which she was handing up into the wagon, she quickly broached the subject.

"Mr Ablett," she said, "I don't s'pose, when you leave for Carson City, you'd consider takin' me along with you?"

"Funny you should ask," replied Ablett. "I was jest sayin' to Mr Stone that we couldn't leave you to make yore own way back to civilisation, that you'd have to ride along with one or other of us."

"Yeah. Wa'al, I'd much prefer to ride along with you," said Sally, favouring him with her warmest smile.

Ray Ablett's heart leapt. The blonde was a mighty good-looking woman, and the thought of being alone with her on the two hundred mile journey to Carson City gave him a pleasant, excited feeling.

"You'll be most welcome to ride along, Miss Sally," he said gallantly.

"Ah, so, you've decided to travel to Carson City with Mr Ablett, have yuh?" enquired Stone, appearing at that moment at the blonde's elbow. He was carrying a crate of whiskey, which he handed up to the saloonkeeper.

"Yes, I have," said Sally.

"I reckon you've made a good decision, for I figure Carson City's yore kinda town," said Stone. Then, turning to the sheriff, who was right behind him, bearing another crate of whiskey, he asked, "Whaddya say, Sheriff?"

"I guess so," said Daniel Budge.

They were loading Ablett's wagon in the small, snow-covered yard at the rear of the Silver Dollar Saloon, and the crate of whiskey, which Budge had brought from the bar-room, proved to be the last of the saloonkeeper's supply of provisions.

"Okay, so what do we load next? Some of yore tables 'n' chairs?" said Stone.

Ray Ablett looked round the wagon and scratched his head.

"There ain't much room left," he muttered. "I reckon we'd best load the piano an' then see what space we've got for tables 'n' chairs."

The Kentuckian smiled sourly and growled, "I was afraid you'd say that."

"Me, too," grinned the young sheriff. "Dunno how in tarnation you expected to load that there piano onto the wagon all on yore own?"

"With the aid of a coupla planks an' a length of rope," replied Ablett.

"Okay," said Stone, "you git the planks an' the rope, an', me an' the sheriff, we'll bring out the piano."

It took Ray Ablett no time at all to find a couple of long planks and lay them at an angle from the ground to the rear of the wagon. The rope he fetched from the stables. And, while he did this Jack Stone and Daniel Budge heaved the piano from the bar-room, through the narrow passage, across the kitchen and out into the yard, Sally McBride and Grey Dove waited and watched. Both had helped in transporting Ray Ablett's possessions from the saloon to the wagon. Now they had nothing more to do, at least until the piano was loaded onto the wagon. Sally climbed up onto the buckboard of the wagon, while the little Paiute girl walked past the stables and towards the barn, where she had left her father's lance, propped against the door.

The loading of the piano onto the wagon went much easier then either Stone or the sheriff had expected. Ray Ablett adjusted the planks so that the piano's four wheels were positioned to run up them. Then, he lassooed the piano with the rope and, climbing onto the wagon, prepared to pull it aboard. With the saloonkeeper pulling and Stone and Budge both pushing, the piano slid smoothly up the planks and onto the wagon.

It was as Ray Ablett was anchoring the piano to one of the wagon's struts, and Jack Stone and Daniel Budge were congratulating themselves on the ease with which they had completed what had promised to be a rather difficult operation, that Grey Dove suddenly let out a sharp cry and came hurrying towards them, the lance grasped tightly in her right hand.

Stone could see, from the terrified look on the girl's face, that something was wrong. He straightway addressed her in her native tongue.

"What is the matter, Grey Dove?" he demanded.

The little Paiute glanced fearfully over her left shoulder.

"I saw a flash of light from over there, on top of those bluffs which overlook the town," she said.

"A flash of light?"

"A reflection."

Stone glanced up into the blue sky. The sun shone brightly. What had it reflected off. A gun barrel, perhaps? Or . . .

"I saw the same reflection just before the bluecoats attacked my village," whispered Grey Dove, her eyes filled with unshed tears.

"Go on," said Stone.

"It was the sun reflecting off the eye-glasses held by the chief of the bluecoats," said Grey Dove.

The sun reflecting off a pair of Army binoculars! Stone swore beneath his breath. Had the troop of US Cavalry returned and was their commander spying on them from the top of the bluff? If the soldiers had returned, it could be for only one reason. Quickly, Stone explained what the girl had seen and what he feared. The others looked again at the Kentuckian.

"But, but, after what the lieutenant said to him, I thought the captain had decided against a shoot-out? Surely, he wouldn't dare?" cried Sally.

"That sonofabitch would dare anythin'," snarled Ablett.

"Not if a court-martial was the inevitable result of his actions," said Stone. "My guess is that, if it is in fact him who is spyin' on us, he's come back with jest a chosen few of his troop, those he can trust to keep their mouths shut."

"But what excuse could he possibly have given for abandonin' the rest of his men?" demanded Sally.

"Dunno. But I'm sure the bastard would have thought of somethin' convincin'," said the Kentuckian.

"So . . . so, what do we do, Mr Stone?" enquired Ablett nervously.

"We carry on loadin' this here wagon with tables 'n' chairs, jest as though we're totally unaware of the soldiers' presence. That way, we have the element of surprise on our side."

"Whaddya reckon their plan is, then?" growled Daniel Budge.

"I expect, once they're satisfied we are quite unsuspectin', they'll come

231

down off them bluffs an' ride into town hell-for-leather, hopin' to hit us 'fore we know what's what."

"You reckon they aim to . . . to kill us!" exclaimed Sally.

"Not you, Miss Sally. Jest the rest of us. I figure they got other plans for you."

"Oh, no!"

Sally gasped and the colour drained slowly from her face.

"Don't worry. It's them that's gonna git killed," said Stone, his face grim and his eyes as hard and as cold as chips of ice.

"But we don't know how many of 'em there are!" cried Ablett.

"Nope. But, before they attack, we will. So, come one, let's continue with loadin' the wagon." Stone smiled at the saloonkeeper and added, "When you go fetch a chair, be sure to bring out yore scattergun at the same time."

Ablett nodded and, jumping down from the wagon, headed for the kitchen door. Daniel Budge and Sally McBride followed. The Kentuckian, however, did not immediately set off after the others. He paused to give Grey Dove a few succinct instructions.

"The bluecoats are coming," he said.

Grey Dove trembled and nodded.

"You guessed as much?"

"Yes."

"This time we are going to be the ones who do the killing. Will you help us?"

The little Paiute's eyes gleamed.

"What shall I do?" she asked.

"Go up the alleyway between the saloon and the neighbouring building, and keep a look-out. My guess is, the bluecoats will assemble on the edge of town. Then, they will charge along Main Street and round the corner of the saloon, hoping to catch us by surprise. They will figure that the snow will, to some extent, deaden the sound of their horses' hooves, enabling them to burst upon us before we realise they are there." Stone smiled at the thirteen-year-old Indian girl and continued, "You will foil this plan. As soon as the bluecoats assemble, you must run back down the alleyway and tell me. And, if you can, let me know their number."

Grey Dove gazed solemnly up at the Kentuckian.

"I shall do as you say," she said quietly, and straight away she was gone.

She ran lightly up the alley, still clutching Two Elks' lance. At the top of the alley, she flattened herself against the side of the saloon and peered cautiously round it into Main Street. The far end of the street lay in the shadows of the bluffs. It was quite deserted, apart from an occasional tumbleweed blowing over the snow, propelled by the fresh March wind. Grey Dove remained at her post, her gaze fixed unwaveringly upon the spot where she expected the horse soldiers to appear.

Stone and the others continued to load the wagon with tables and chairs from the bar-room. But, leaning against the side of the wagon, were Stone's and the sheriffs Winchesters and Ray Ablett's shotgun, all three loaded and ready for use. Stone checked his Frontier Model Colt and Budge checked his Colt Peacemaker, while Ray Ablett produced an ancient Webly R.I.C. revolver and a small, two-barrelled Derringer. The latter he handed to Sally.

The wait seemed endless. Indeed, there was no space left on the wagon for the loading of any more furniture, and still the soldiers had not made their move. Stone was beginning to wonder whether Grey Dove had been mistaken, or whether, perhaps, there was a perfectly innocent explanation for the reflection she had seen. It was as that thought crossed the Kentuckian's mind that Grey Dove suddenly began running back down the alleyway. She ran up to him and gasped breathlessly, "They are coming!"

"It's the same bluecoats?"

"Yes."

"How many?"

"Seven, including their chief."

"Okay, let's git to our positions!"

The others needed no second telling. Stone and the sheriff crouched down at either side of the wagon, while Ablett and the blonde clambered up onto it and ducked down among the provisions, their guns aimed over the buckboard towards the alley. Grey Dove, meantime, hid round the corner of the saloon, beside the kitchen door, her young face frightened yet determined, and the lance held tightly with both hands.

Captain George Riley and his men galloped furiously through the ghost town, their horses' hooves kicking up puffs of snow as they raced along. Riley had surveyed their intended victims from the heights of the bluffs and observed them busily engaged in loading the saloonkeeper's wagon. Assuming them to be unaware of his presence, he was supremely confident of success. Exultantly, he drew his revolver, while his men pulled their carbines from their saddleboots.

The seven riders swerved into the alley between the saloon and the barbering parlour, and hurtled down it at full pelt. George Riley led the way, his men bunched up close behind him in twos. They sped between the two buildings towards the wagon standing in the snow-covered yard. And, so fast did they ride, it was not until Riley was within a few yards of the wagon that any of them realised there was nobody engaged in loading it.

It was at that moment that Stone and the others opened fire. The result was devastating. The Kentuckian's Frontier Model Colt barked thrice and three riders were blasted from their saddles. Captain Riley was hit in the chest, while, immediately behind him, both Corporal Joe Shaughnessy and the negro, Bass, were struck in the belly. Daniel Budge was the next to fire, and he was no less lethal. Three other troopers were toppled from their horses. Devlin was shot in the head and killed outright, while the huge, bearish troopers, Rickard and Fallon, like their captain, suffered severe chest wounds. Only Trooper Stark managed to rein in his horse unscathed, as Ray Ablett's revolver shots whistled harmlessly past his ear.

Stark's luck did not last, however. As he struggled to wheel his horse round in the narrow alleyway, Jack Stone quickly exchanged his revolver for his rifle. Bringing the Winchester to bear on the trooper, Stone fired at the man's retreating figure. The slug thudded into the trooper's back and, passing through his body, erupted out of his chest. Stark screamed, threw his arms in the air and fell backwards off his horse and onto the snow, where he lay twitching, his life's blood slowly oozing out of him.

Of the others, Joe Shaughnessy was the first to stagger to his feet. He had lost his carbine during the course of his fall, and was clutching his belly with one hand, in a vain effort to prevent his guts from spilling out of the huge hole in his stomach. His ugly features were contorted into an amalgam of anguish and rage, and he attempted to draw the revolver from his holster. Then, just as he finally managed to pull the gun clear, Ray Ablett fired again, this time with the shotgun. The saloonkeeper emptied both barrels at point blank range and the blast cut the corporal in two.

Bass, no longer the smiling negro, crawled across the snow towards the wagon, leaving a trail of blood and guts behind him. He had somehow succeeded in regaining hold of his carbine and murder was in his heart. But, before he could aim and squeeze the trigger, the first of Sally McBride's shots rang out. Whether by luck or not, the bullet struck the negro plumb in the centre of his forehead, drilling a neat hole in his skull and entering his brain. Bass gasped, released his grip on the carbine and slumped forward in the snow.

Rickard and Fallon were the next to attempt to rise. Both had suffered extremely bad chest wounds and only their immense strength and incredible toughness got them to their feet. Swearing roundly, they drew their revolvers and blasted a couple of shots at their ambushers. One shot buried itself in a sack of corn, inches from Ray Ablett's head, while the other nicked a hole in the top of Daniel Budge's Stetson. The response was deadly. Rickard was hit by forty-five calibre slugs from both Stone and the sheriff, and his fellow-trooper was struck by Sally McBride's second shot. This time the blonde was not so accurate in her shooting, the bullet merely clipping Fallon's arm. A final shot from the Kentuckian finished him off.

Of the seven would-be killers, six were dead. Only their leader remained alive. Slowly, Captain George Riley clambered to his feet. He clutched at his chest, where Stone's bullet had punctured it just beneath the collar-bone. A trickle of blood oozed out from between his fingers. His face was unnaturally pale, yet his cruel black eyes continued to glitter venomously.

"Wa'al," he drawled, "what are you gonna do now?"

"Whaddya mean?" rasped Stone, as he and Daniel Budge approached the officer, their revolvers aimed directly at his heart.

"I mean, you surely don't aim to shoot an unarmed man?" said Riley, and he grinned contemptuously at the two men.

"I'm sure tempted," said Stone, "But I guess not."

"That's right. We don't kill in cold blood," said Budge.

"So, we call it a truce, huh?" sneered Riley.

"I dunno 'bout that. I reckon . . ."

But Stone got no further. He was interrupted by a piercing scream from somewhere behind his left shoulder, and, before he could prevent her, Grey Dove rushed past him and, with a strength way beyond her thirteen years, plunged Two Elks' lance into the bluecoated captain's body. The razor-sharp head went clean through him, like a knife through butter, and, with a hideous cry, he fell backwards.

There he lay, pinned to the ground, his heels beating a silent tattoo in the snow. That Riley was in dire agony, there was absolutely no doubt. Daniel Budge stepped forward to pull the lance from his body, but Stone held him back.

"No," snarled the Kentuckian. "Let the bastard suffer!"

He placed a large, comforting hand upon Grey Dove's shoulder. She stood over the dying man, trembling with emotion. Tears coursed down her young face, as she stared down at her father's murderer.

Stone smiled grimly.

"Vengeance is sweet," he said.

FIGHTING RAMROD
Charles N. Heckelmann

Most men would have cut their losses, but Frazer counted the bullets in his guns and said he'd soak the range in blood before he'd give up another inch of what was his.

LONE GUN
Eric Allen

Smoke Blackbird had been away too long. The Lequires had seized the Blackbird farm, forcing the Indians and settlers off, and no one seemed willing to fight! He had to fight alone.

THE THIRD RIDER
Barry Cord

Mel Rawlins wasn't going to let anything stand in his way. His father was murdered, his two brothers gone. Now Mel rode for vengeance.

ARIZONA DRIFTERS
W. C. Tuttle

When drifting Dutton and Lonnie Steelman decide to become partners they find that they have a common enemy in the formidable Thurston brothers.

TOMBSTONE
Matt Braun

Wells Fargo paid Luke Starbuck to outgun the silver-thieving stagecoach gang at Tombstone. Before long Luke can see the only thing bearing fruit in this eldorado will be the gallows tree.

HIGH BORDER RIDERS
Lee Floren

Buckshot McKee and Tortilla Joe cut the trail of a border tough who was running Mexican beef into Texas. They stopped the smuggler in his tracks.

BRETT RANDALL, GAMBLER
E. B. Mann

Larry Day had the choice of running away from the law or of assuming a dead man's place. No matter what he decided he was bound to end up dead.

THE GUNSHARP
William R. Cox

The Eggerleys weren't very smart. They trained their sights on Will Carney and Arizona's biggest blood bath began.

THE DEPUTY OF SAN RIANO
Lawrence A. Keating and
Al. P. Nelson

When a man fell dead from his horse, Ed Grant was spotted riding away from the scene. The deputy sheriff rode out after him and came up against everything from gunfire to dynamite.

FARGO: MASSACRE RIVER
John Benteen

The ambushers up ahead had now blocked the road. Fargo's convoy was a jumble, a perfect target for the insurgents' weapons!

SUNDANCE: DEATH IN THE LAVA
John Benteen

The Modoc's captured the wagon train and its cargo of gold. But now the halfbreed they called Sundance was going after it . . .

HARSH RECKONING
Phil Ketchum

Five years of keeping himself alive in a brutal prison had made Brand tough and careless about who he gunned down . . .

FARGO: PANAMA GOLD
John Benteen

With foreign money behind him, Buckner was going to destroy the Panama Canal before it could be completed. Fargo's job was to stop Buckner.

FARGO:
THE SHARPSHOOTERS
John Benteen

The Canfield clan, thirty strong were raising hell in Texas. Fargo was tough enough to hold his own against the whole clan.

PISTOL LAW
Paul Evan Lehman

Lance Jones came back to Mustang for just one thing — revenge! Revenge on the people who had him thrown in jail.